Firefight

Target
Hostage
Renegade

Firefight

BY ALEX WHEELER

SCHOLASTIC INC.

New York Toronto London Auckland Sydney Mexico City New Delhi Hong Kong

www.starwars.com
www.scholastic.com

ISBN-13: 978-0-545-14084-3
ISBN-10: 0-545-14084-6

12 11 10 9 8 7 6 5 4 3 2 1   9 10 11 12 13 14/0

Book design by Rick DeMonico
Cover illustrations by Randy Martinez
Printed in the U.S.A.
First printing, September 2009

Ten points of light shot through the midnight black, streaking toward the ground like falling stars.

Make a wish.

It was a woman's voice, soft and kind, fluttering up from a dark, buried place in his mind. Another man might have taken it as a long-forgotten voice from a long-forgotten past.

But X-7 had no past.

And these were no stars.

He shook off the imagined voice, the echo of an echo of a memory. Long ago, in the beginning, he'd heard voices like this, closed his eyes and seen strangely familiar faces smiling down on him, breathed in a hint of fresh spiceloaf or the rich scent of overripe blumfruits floating on a warm breeze and felt that other life, that *human* life, nearly close enough to touch. There had been a time when he'd held tight to these memories that weren't memories, this evidence that he'd once been someone else. That he'd once been *someone*.

But that had been before. He'd learned. His Commander had taught him. Memories were wrong; the past was dead. He wasn't someone; he was no one, and that was right. That was good. The Commander had relieved him of the burdens of the past, the pangs of memory, the frailties of emotion and human need. X-7 had only one need: to obey his Commander, and that, too, was right.

That was good.

Except he had failed. Luke Skywalker lived, though the Commander wanted him dead.

And now X-7 had failed again.

"Return to base for retraining," his master had commanded. But X-7 had disobeyed. X-7, who lived to serve, who had no life, no purpose, no will beyond the desires of his Commander, had defied the call, had fled to this lifeless moon on the fringes of the galaxy, had made a new plan.

It was not disobedience, he told himself. It was not a fear of the retraining, with its long needles and neuronic whips and dark cells and pain. It was Skywalker. X-7 couldn't return to his master in failure and shame, not while Skywalker still breathed. X-7 never killed for fun or in rage; he killed only for his Commander. But there was something about the young Rebel, something that made X-7 boil. X-7 couldn't — *wouldn't* — return to his master until the mission was complete and Skywalker was dead.

It was the right thing. It was the good thing.

But then why were the voices of the past returning to haunt him? Why was the dead hollow inside him slowly filling with anger, with the need to see Skywalker dead?

The Commander was right; X-7 knew that. Something inside him was wrong. There were impurities that needed to be scrubbed away. Erased. X-7 had tried to ignore that, and now he was being punished. *I will go back. I will obey,* he promised himself. *As soon as Skywalker is dead.*

"Targets incoming," the perimeter alert system informed him. X-7 shook off his doubts. The time had come. Ten lights blipped across the target scope. Through the moon base's transparisteel roof, he watched the ships approach. Ten of the galaxy's most skilled, most determined, most ruthless pilots, all eager to carry out his wishes. He had taken his time composing the team, but the frustrating wait was nearly over. They had come to Iope, the third moon of Rinn, with the promise of a mysterious job and rewards beyond their wildest dreams if they accomplished the mission. Pilots like these didn't ask questions; they just chased the payoff.

Some of them, the worthy ones, might even receive it.

"I'll meet your ships at the landing site," he said to them, transmitting a set of coordinates. "Good luck." He shut down the comm before they could ask why they would need luck. They wouldn't. Only skill. The ones who had enough of it would have their answer soon. As for the ones who lacked it . . . they'd have their answer even sooner.

He activated the laser-cannon targeting computer and zeroed in on the ten points of light. "Welcome to Iope," he said.

Then he fired.

"Blast it!" Slis Tieeer Dualli swung his CloakShape fighter hard to starboard. His insectoid compound eyes took in every inch of the battlefield at once while the eye on the back of his head scanned the radar screens erected behind him. A bolt of laserfire blazed past his cockpit, too close for comfort. He couldn't believe that the kriff-ing mudcrutch was *firing* at him!

In his twenty-year career as a mercenary, Dualli had met his fair share of galactic scum. But it never failed to enrage him. He took their money, yes. He flew their missions. Smuggled their goods. Assassinated their ene-mies. And he waited. Waited for them to step over the line, to cross him one too many times, to make a mistake that couldn't be forgiven. Dualli was the best pilot in the Outer Rim; everyone knew that. And he was the best Kobok pilot in the galaxy. But few were bold enough to hire him.

Probably because half of his employers ended up corpses.

Dualli wasn't picky about his jobs. So when the mysterious human had lured him with the promise of a rich reward, he'd come eagerly. But he had also come prepared.

He increased power to the deflector shields and armed a concussion missile. One direct hit would be enough to destroy his traitorous employer's base. And Dualli's modified launchers carried six missiles each. He could probably go a good ways toward destroying the moon itself. Either way, the human who'd made the mistake of firing on him would soon be in pieces. He just needed to approach close enough for a clear shot.

In their original form, CloakShapes were known for their sluggish maneuvering abilities. But no one who knew anything about flying would be caught dead in an original CloakShape. Dualli's had been modified with a rear-mounted maneuvering fin and a turbocharged ion engine. They'd rescued him from plenty of tight spots — far tighter than this.

The Kobok eased the ship into a shallow descent. A barrage of laserfire rained down on him, scorching the hull. Red light flickered on his monitor as the power generator caught a glancing blow. Whoever this human was, he was good. Too bad for him Dualli was better.

The attacks intensified as Dualli neared the surface. His hands dancing across the control panel, he guided the ship through the hail of laser bolts. The dull, pitted plain of the moon came into view, a transparisteel-domed base rising at the edge of a long ravine. "Got you," Dualli muttered.

The alert system screamed as a missile hurtled straight toward the CloakShape. Dualli veered away from the surface, nearly crashing into a Preybird flying just overhead. "Blast you!" Dualli screamed into the comm. "Get out of my flight path!" He yanked his controls to the left, and the ship peeled off hard to port, narrowly avoiding a collision — and taking him straight into the line of fire. A laser bolt sizzled into the ship's underbelly. The ship shuddered, and a moment later, the hyperdrive monitor shorted out. The shot had cooked his drive generator, which meant he was stuck in this blasted system until he could fix it — or acquire another ship.

Dualli fixed his glare on the clumsy Preybird. Once he'd taken care of his traitorous employer, the incompetent pilot would be next.

The near miss might have made another pilot more careful; it only made Dualli more impatient. He took the ship into a steep dive and sharply leveled out at one thousand meters. He increased power to his thrusters and adjusted his targeting computer. The base loomed in his scope. Then Dualli opened a comlink to the surface. He wanted the human to know that he was about to die — and that Dualli would be responsible.

He would have preferred creeping up behind the enemy and jabbing a venomous claw into his neck. But payback from a distance would have to do. "This is Slis Tieeer Dualli," he announced. "Say good-bye, because this is your last moment to live."

The answer came back in Dualli's native tongue. "*Chsthiss,* Slis Tieeer Dualli." *Good-bye.*

Light blazed from the surface of the planet, two klicks from the base Dualli had targeted. It took Dualli only a few seconds to process the situation and reorient his targeting computer. But a few seconds was one too many. The surface-to-air proton torpedo slammed the CloakShape fighter's deflector shield generator.

The shields went down completely, laying Dualli bare to the enemy attack. He flicked a spindly yellow arm toward the escape-pod activation switch, but nothing happened. Total system malfunction — the CloakShape was dying.

Laserfire strafed the ship. Dualli glimpsed orange flickers with his third eye as flames licked at the cockpit.

"*Chsthiss,*" Dualli had time to whisper as another torpedo screamed toward him.

The CloakShape exploded.

The *Leilana's Dagger* bounced and shuddered in the rain of debris from the exploding CloakShape fighter. Jayn threw power to the front deflectors, praying that the ion-flux stabilizers would keep him from spinning out of control. A chunk of the CloakShape spiraled into the distance, disappearing in the black. *I could be next,* Jayn thought, trying to keep his hands from shaking. It wasn't like him to get rattled on the job, even in an ambush. But this time was different.

Just one last job. That was what he'd told himself. For years Leilana had begged him to settle planetside, live a nice quiet life with her. A *safe* life. He'd put her off, again and again. *Next year,* he'd told her. *Next job.* But now Leilana was gone.

He'd missed his chance to do the right thing by Leilana. One last job, one last payment, and he'd have enough to move them to Laressa, Phindar's capital city, where they could have the life they deserved. But the job wasn't exactly working out as he'd planned.

Two of the other ships had already peeled out of orbit and winked into hyperdrive. Jayn decided to follow them. He could do without the credits. He would find a way to make things work in Laressa. He could find a nice, boring job ferrying rich guys to and from their rich homes. He could do anything if he could just maneuver out of here. He plotted a course out of orbit, zigzagging through space to avoid the laserfire. Debris pummeled the shields, but the freighter could take it. As long as —

"No!" Jayn shouted as a burst of laserfire took out his port ion engine. He increased power to the thrusters, but a plume of flame shot from his main drive nozzles. The ship vibrated beneath him, as if it were about to fly apart. He tried to pull up, to avoid an incoming blast, but the controls were nonresponsive. A torpedo blasted the reinforced hull. He heard an alarming metallic scream, and moments later a sizable chunk of his starboard wing floated past his cockpit. The *Leilana's Dagger* began to drift.

"No," Jayn said again, slamming a fist into his useless control panel. "No. No. No!"

The engines were toast. And according to the monitors, fires raged throughout the ship, causing multiple systems failures. Weapons. Navigation. Deflector shields. He was dead in the air. Laserfire pounded the defenseless ship. Acrid smoke billowed into the cockpit. *I'm sorry*, he thought, choking in the thick, foul air.

Don't be sorry. It was Leilana's voice. *At least now we can be together.*

He smiled. As the storm of fire consumed him, he searched for her face in the flames. But there was only light and pain.

And then darkness.

Div pulled his ship into a steep dive, dodging the whirling storm of flak. Laserfire streaked past the cockpit. He veered starboard, angling the ship away from the barrage of fire, but took a glancing hit on his port wing. The deflector shields were taking a beating. Another hit and he'd be cooked.

Then it's simple, Div thought coolly. *I won't let it happen again.*

Three of the other ships had exploded before his eyes. Two more had fled. If the job had paid any less, perhaps Div would have followed them. But he needed the credits — and he was more than a little interested in meeting the man who'd set him up.

So he steered calmly through the laserfire and debris, letting his instincts take over. The ship dipped and rolled, spun and corkscrewed, tracing an intricate path of steep dives and hairpin turns. Nothing could touch him.

His ship was hot off the assembly line, one of the first of KSE's revamped Firespray line. It had been a serious indulgence, but it had been worth it. With its rotating twin blaster cannons and rotating cockpit, it was easily the most graceful and powerful ship he'd ever flown.

After only two months, it was like an extension of his own body, and he had no doubts that he could land it safely.

Now! he thought suddenly, and without questioning the impulse, he pulled up into a steep ascent — as another stream of laserfire sizzled through the space he'd just occupied.

Div smiled. *You want to kill me, you'll have to try a little harder,* he thought.

The domed transparisteel base was the obvious target. Too obvious. And the pilot of the CloakShape had fallen for it. Div didn't intend to suffer the same fate.

The laserfire explosions bursting from the surface were clearly traceable to the base, even with the naked eye. To open fire from an undisguised and undefended surface base? It reeked of incompetence. And Div's gut told him that his would-be employer was far from incompetent.

He keyed a new command into his computer, instructing it to triangulate the beams of laserfire, tracing them back to their point of origin. The calculations would have been difficult even if he were sitting still; speeding through space, navigating with wild gyrations to avoid the flak and fire, made them nearly impossible. But the near impossible was Div's specialty, and soon his suspicions were confirmed. The fire coming from the base was just a cover. The computer's triangulation directed him to an apparently empty spot two klicks from the moon base. A preliminary recon sweep indicated nothing but a rocky embankment. As Div drew the ship dangerously close to the surface, however, it became clear that the rocks were camouflaging a primary weapons embankment.

The moon had no atmosphere, which meant no cloud cover to fog Div's view of the ground. Soon he'd drawn near enough to spot the laser cannons. Dodging and weaving through the streaking fire, he shut down his targeting computer. It could do the job, but sometimes Div preferred handling things himself. He liked the feel of the targeting controls in his hands, liked letting his instincts take over and guide him toward a sure hit. Liked, most of all, that moment of *knowing*, when the target was in position and he could fire.

He took his time lining up the shots. It was as if a calm eye had opened up in the storm of laserfire, letting him aim in peace. But the calm was only an illusion. Div was still dancing between the beams, avoiding debris and sliding back and forth through crisscrossing webs of light. He moved as if the world had slowed to a crawl for him, as if the evasive maneuvers were beneath his notice. He saved his focus, his energy, for the shot.

He lined up the first laser cannon with his sights.

Fired.

Direct hit.

The laser cannon embankment exploded.

Div squeezed the trigger a second time, then a third. And in an instant, the cannons were silenced, the skies clear. Smoke mushroomed from the ground. As it dissipated, a small figure emerged. Div was still too high up to make out any features, but he imagined that the man was gazing directly at him.

The ground parted, revealing a wide manufactured cavern beneath the moon's surface. An underground hangar.

Now that it was safe, the other four ships came in for a landing. Div waited until they were all on the ground before joining them. Their employer had gathered the best pilots in the galaxy, but now they would all know that Div was the best of the best. The one to whom they owed their lives.

The moment his ship touched down in the hangar, Div grabbed his blaster. He hadn't made it through one ambush only to walk unarmed into another. But when he exited the ship, the other four pilots were assembled in a line, no weapons in sight. Two were humanoid males, one human and one Sorrusian, both grizzled and wearing identical hostile grimaces. The third was a Chistori, with beady black eyes and jagged teeth gnashing in his long, narrow snout. While the other pilots, like Div, draped themselves in simple, loose-fitting fabrics for easy maneuvering, the Chistori was in full body armor. It likely contained a temperature-control system,

Div decided. Chistori were cold-blooded; without accommodation, drastic temperature changes could be deadly for them.

The final pilot, a human woman with short, spiky black hair and tattoos inked across her face, barely acknowledged his presence. Her eyes were riveted on the fifth figure, unmistakably the man in charge. He stood off to the side and appraised them all with an icy stare. As Div joined them, the man began to clap, a humorless smile on his face. "Nice work," he said, nodding toward the destroyed laser cannons.

Div aimed his blaster. "You want to tell me why you just tried to blow me out of the sky?"

The man's smile widened. It was a gruesome mockery of human emotion. "Merely a test to separate the quinto wheat from the chaff. I'm investing a significant amount of money into this mission. I had to ensure I'd chosen correctly. I assume you're still interested in my job offer?"

Div holstered the weapon. He had no doubt that he had sharper reflexes than anyone there. If things went sour, he could protect himself. And he had the "significant amount of money" to consider. "I'm here, aren't I?"

The man handed each of the pilots a datapad. "Gentlemen and lady, your target is a man named Luke Skywalker. He works with the Rebellion —"

Div's hand inched toward his blaster. "This is an *Imperial* job?"

The man shook his head. "Strictly freelance," he said. "The Empire may have its reasons for wanting Skywalker dead; I wouldn't know. I have my own."

Div could usually tell when people were lying, but this man defied his instincts. His face was a blank, free of the almost imperceptible tells — tightened muscles, dilating pupils, twitching eyelids — that gave most liars away. Div chose to believe him. For now.

"You want him dead so bad, why not kill him yourself?" Div asked.

The man stiffened. "Because I choose to hire you to do it," he said tightly. "I suggest that be your last question."

The other pilots glared at Div. Div glared back.

"The Rebels have a tight security net around Skywalker," the man continued. "When he's on the ground, he's usually untouchable, which is why you're all here. Skywalker fancies himself a hotshot pilot. I'm wagering that at least one of you is better." He nodded at their datapads. "All the information you need is in there, including details of his upcoming mission and intercept coordinates. You'll operate as a team and split the money evenly. Payment only if and when Skywalker dies."

The Sorrusian threw his datapad to the ground. "*Team?* I work alone," he snarled. "I don't need anyone's help to take down a *human*. And I can prove it."

He reached for his blaster — and dropped to the ground before his fingers could even graze the holster. A thin trail of smoke wafted up from the neat hole through his forehead.

Their employer held his blaster casually, almost carelessly, as if it were a toy. Div couldn't help being impressed. Speed, accuracy, and ruthless efficiency: It was a formidable combination.

"Anyone else have any concerns they'd like to raise?" the man asked.

The remaining pilots shook their heads, exchanging wary glances. Div spoke. "Say we work as a team. Who's in charge?"

Their employer glanced toward the rubble of the laser cannons. "You don't seem like the kind of man to avoid the obvious," he said, then turned back to the other pilots. "Grish B'reen," he said flatly, nodding as the Chistori straightened up. "Fallon Pollo," he said, and the grizzled man gave him a sarcastic salute. "Clea Sook." The woman met his gaze without flinching.

He clapped Div on the shoulder. "Pilots, meet Lune Divinian. Your new leader."

Yavin 4 to Skywalker, Yavin 4 to Skywalker. Come in, Skywalker." There was a long silence. "Hello? Anyone home, kid?" Han Solo teased, rapping his knuckles gently against Luke's head.

Luke jumped, finally noticing Han's presence. He'd been sitting on the floor with his eyes closed for the past hour; he wondered how long Han had been watching.

Han grinned. "Taking your naps sitting up now?"

"Not exactly." Luke flushed. He'd been trying to meditate, to open himself up to the power of the Force. It was something he'd seen Obi-Wan Kenobi do. Inaction could sometimes be as powerful as action, old Ben had explained. Unfortunately, he'd never explained exactly what that meant. So Luke had sat down, closed his eyes, and waited for the Force to give him some answers. *Where can I find X-7? Why is he trying to kill me? How could I have been so dumb as to believe he was my friend?*

But the Force had been silent. He might as well have taken a nap.

"What is this, then?" Han asked. "More of your Jedi mumbo jumbo?"

"It's not mumbo — oh, forget it." He wasn't embarrassed to be caught exploring his Jedi skills — even if it had turned out to be a total failure. But none of Luke's friends realized just how desperate he was to track down X-7, and he wanted to keep it that way. Everyone was eager to find the assassin, of course. As long as he was alive, Luke was in danger. But for Luke, it was more than that. He was angry. The man who'd called himself Tobin Elad, the man who'd revealed himself to be an Imperial assassin, had pretended to be a friend. He'd weaseled his way into Luke's life and trust, and Luke couldn't forget it.

Nor could he forgive.

But the trail had gone cold, and the Force was no help — which meant Luke had to wait for X-7 to come to him. Something told Luke it was bound to happen. Soon.

"Commander Narra wants us in Base One," Han said. "But if you want me to tell him you're too tired . . ."

"Let's go," Luke said, eager for the distraction.

When they arrived at the looming Great Temple that served as the Rebel base station, Wedge Antilles, Zev Senesca, and Chewbacca were already waiting in the briefing room. Commander Arhul Narra nodded as

Luke and Han took their seats at the table. "Good, we can begin," he said brusquely. His protocol droid, K-3PO, activated an overhead screen. It lit with the image of a planet, inky storm clouds swirling in the planet's atmosphere.

"This is Kamino," Narra said as images of churning seas and weeping skies flickered across the screen. In the distance, Luke could make out shadowy stilt cities shrouded by fog. "It's on the edges of Wild Space, but unlike most of the planets out there, Kamino is valued by the Empire. Its scientists played a crucial role in the Emperor's rise to power."

"Sure, they made the clones," Zev said. "Why the history lesson, boss? Even the Empire finally figured out that natural borns make better fighters."

Narra looked out over the faces of the pilots, all too young to have served in the Clone Wars. "I fought side by side with those . . . *things*," he said, "before Palpatine turned them against the Republic. Those Kaminoan scientists created a living, breathing, deadly weapon that nearly destroyed us all. And now we have reports that they may have created another."

Jumbled fuzzy images of a laboratory appeared on the screen. "For several months, we've been aware of a secret Imperial research base on Kamino. The scientists were said to be developing some kind of superweapon. We've tried to infiltrate the lab, with no success. But one month ago, with no warning or explanation, the base was abandoned by the Empire." He gestured toward K-3PO, who deactivated the screen. "You'll access the base, gather any information you can about the weapons developed there — and, of course, scavenge any equipment or artillery that might be useful to the Rebellion. I've uploaded the mission details to your datapads. You leave tonight."

"Oh, do we?" Han said. "That's it? You're not even going to say please?"

"Han!" Luke chided him. Commander Narra was the leader of Red Squadron and Renegade Flight. Luke was no longer as intimidated by him as he used to be, but something about the man still commanded respect. He'd been a warrior for nearly his entire life and had single-handedly rebuilt Red Squadron after it had almost been demolished in the Battle of Yavin.

"It's all right," Narra said. "As I was about to say, we're down several members of the squadron at the moment. Captain Solo and Chewbacca, if you could contribute your services in their stead, the Rebel Alliance would be grateful."

"Well, the *Millennium Falcon*'s got a busted acceleration compensator, so it's not like I'm going anywhere anytime soon. And since you asked so *nicely* . . ." Han shot Luke a smug grin. Then he slapped his hands on the table and rose to his feet. "I'm all yours."

• • •

C-3PO tottered in nervous circles around his astromech counterpart, R2-D2, ensuring that everything was in working order. "You take care of Master Luke, now," he instructed the little droid sternly. "And don't do anything foolish." C-3PO would be traveling with Leia on a diplomatic mission to Mon Calamari while R2-D2 headed to Kamino with Luke.

R2-D2 beeped indignantly. He was doing a last-minute check of Luke's X-wing, tweaking the calibration on the flashback suppressor.

"Because I know you," C-3PO pointed out. "And you're always taking silly risks."

R2-D2 whirred and whistled.

"Me?" C-3PO slapped his bronzium hand to his chest. "Of course *I'll* be careful. *I'm* always careful."

"Come on, Artoo," Luke said, joining the droids. Han and Leia trailed him. "We should go."

"Master Luke, I don't like the sound of this mission," C-3PO informed him. "Surely the Empire had a good reason for abandoning that base."

"I'm sure they did, Threepio," Luke agreed. "And we're going to find out what it is."

R2-D2 beeped eagerly.

"See?" Luke said. "Artoo thinks the mission sounds like a great idea."

"Oh, of course he does," C-3PO said in disgust. He flicked a hand at R2-D2. "Go, then. Just make sure you come back in one piece."

Leia rested a comforting hand on C-3PO. "Artoo will be just fine," she assured him. "Don't worry."

"I would never do such a thing, Your Highness," C-3PO said. "I have absolute faith in Master Luke." But when Luke and R2-D2 turned to ready the X-wing, he followed them nervously, already jabbering more useless warnings and advice.

Han burst into laughter. "Crazy bucket of bolts."

"He's worried about his friend," Leia said, irritated. Han could turn anything into a joke. "I think it's sweet."

"Oh yeah?" Han raised his eyebrows. "And how about you, Princess?"

"How about me what?" But she knew what.

"Pretty dangerous mission I'm heading out on," Han said. "You want to give me any last-minute warnings? Beg me to come back in one piece? Tell me not to go?"

Dangerous? Leia forced a laugh. It wasn't that she wished Luke and Han weren't going on the mission. The Rebellion needed them. She just wished she were going with them. Just in case. The meeting on Mon Calamari was crucial to maintaining the stability of the Alliance; she knew that. But she couldn't shake the feeling that she belonged on the other side of the galaxy, with Han and Luke. "The base has been abandoned. This mission's about as dangerous as a game of sabacc."

"Then lucky thing you're not going," Han shot back. At Leia's look of confusion, he explained himself. "Because you're terrible at bluffing, Highness."

She rolled her eyes, determined to admit nothing.

"No need to be embarrassed," he said. "It's only natural. You put a little space between you and something that matters to you, of course you're going to think about worst-case scenarios. In fact . . ." He shifted his gaze to the ground, as if afraid to meet her eyes. "You'll be gone all week on Mon Calamari, right?"

"That's the plan," Leia said, surprised. Was Han about to admit that he worried about *her* safety? She smiled. It was just like him, teasing her about her feelings when really he was just embarrassed about having any of his own. "Is something bothering you?"

He rubbed his temples, visibly agitated. "I just don't like it, that's all."

"Yes?" Leia prompted him, suppressing a smile. "Don't like what?"

"Leaving behind . . . my ship."

"Your ship?" Leia echoed, incredulous. "Your *ship*?"

"Sure. Chewie's coming with me, and you're not even going to be around to keep an eye on her, and it just doesn't feel right, leaving her behind all alone like this."

"Right," Leia said in a flat voice. "You'll worry about *her* while you're gone. Of course."

"What?" Han asked, finally picking up on her anger.

"Nothing," Leia said. "Absolutely nothing. Just . . ." She shook her head and waved an arm toward the *Millennium Falcon*. "Go," she told him. "I'm heading out soon. So why don't you go say good-bye to your precious *ship*."

He shrugged, then started to walk away. "Oh, and by the way, Your Worshipfulness . . ." He paused, his back still to Leia. "Try not to get yourself killed out there."

Leia sighed. "You, too, Han." But she said it too quietly for him to hear.

pproaching Kamino orbit," Han said into the comm. "You copy, Luke — uh, I mean, Red Leader?"

"Copy that." Luke's response came in just as the other four X-wings winked out of hyperspace, back into normal space.

An enormous gray globe loomed before them, its atmosphere roiling with storm clouds. There were no Star Destroyers circling the planet, nothing at all to indicate an Imperial presence. But Han still felt something dark and dangerous emanating from the planet. Maybe it was the thought of all those Kamino assembly lines churning out stormtroopers like a nerf-sausage factory. Or maybe it was just the thought of all that rain. Han hated rain.

He rubbed his shoulder blades and did his best to straighten up in the cramped cockpit. These X-wings maneuvered well, no doubt about that. But they were no replacement for the *Millennium Falcon*. For one thing, what good was a ship without a decent-sized hold where you could enjoy a game of dejarik and a bottle of lum? Still, it could be worse, Han reminded himself. He could be a Wookiee.

"You still with us, pal?" he asked on a private com-link to Chewbacca. "Enjoying your luxury liner?"

The Wookiee growled angrily in return. Han laughed, remembering how ridiculous Chewie had looked hunched up in his X-wing, fur matted against the cock-pit windows. X-wings, like most everything else built to human scale, just weren't made for Wookiees.

A light began flashing on the main screen of Han's X-wing. "Luke, my ship's picking up some strange gravi-tational readings," he reported.

"Copy that," Luke replied. "Wedge and Zev reported them, too."

"Probably just a natural fluctuation in the gravi-tational field," Han said. "I've seen this kind of thing before. Nothing to worry about."

Luke paused. "I don't know," he said. "I have a bad feeling about this."

Han rolled his eyes. Luke and his bad feelings. . . . He knew that Luke thought it was the "Force" giving him some kind of warning. The kid refused to accept that everyone had *feelings*. Sometimes it was instinct; some-times it was luck. Sometimes it was just a bad batch of won-won. Anything but a mystical, invisible galactic *Force* imparting wisdom from beyond.

"There's a clear path to the surface," Han said. "We go in now, we can be on the ground in —"

"Hold on," Luke said. "I want to investigate these gravitational readings. Something's not right."

Han shook his head. The kid was being overcautious. "It's not necessary, Luke. I told you —"

"*Red Two*, hold your course until further notice," Luke said, with special emphasis on the call sign. "Red Leader out."

"What was Narra thinking, putting Luke in control of this mission?" Han mumbled on his private line to Chewie. Not that Luke wasn't an amazing pilot; he'd proven that he was. But the kid was green.

Chewbacca shot back a short burst of barks and woofs.

"Fine, so I don't like taking orders from *anyone*," Han admitted. "The only person who *can* tell me what to do is —"

Chewbacca interrupted with an alarmed bark.

"The *Empire*?" Han repeated, incredulous. "Since when do I let the Empire tell me what to do?"

Chewbacca barked again, and then Han's radar screen lit up with lights.

"Incoming!" Wedge Antilles shouted through the comm unit.

"Who are these guys?" Zev asked as a motley collection of ships appeared before them. Han spotted a couple of freighters, a Preybird, and what looked like a Firespray. "They don't look Imperial."

A blast of laserfire shot from the cannons of the Firespray, straight for Luke's ship. He banked sharply to port just in time.

"They don't look friendly, whoever they are!" Han shouted, increasing power to his front deflectors and accelerating toward the nearest freighter. "I say we take them out . . . unless you have different orders, *Red Leader*?"

"Your orders are not to get toasted, Red Two," Luke said. "And that goes for all of you, Red Squadron. Let's show these guys they're making a *big* mistake!"

Han unfolded the wings of his ship and locked S-foils in attack position. The rest of the squadron did the same, gearing up for battle.

"Stay on my wing, Chewie," Han said into the comm, taking off after the nearest ship. He adjusted his targeting computer, waiting for the Preybird to edge into the center of the scope. Then he squeezed the trigger, launching a missile at the enemy ship. "Take that — *whoa!*"

The Preybird shot an antiballistic countermeasure from its tail launcher. It collided with the missile, unleashing an enormous explosion. Han pulled up hard, nearly sucked into the fireball. The nose of the X-wing glowed white with heat. And the Preybird was already looping around, closing in on Han for a kill shot.

Suddenly, a shower of laserfire raked across its hull. Han glanced up to see Chewbacca's X-wing streaking past. The Wookiee had bought him a few seconds, just enough time to shake the Preybird and regroup.

Five X-wings, four enemy ships: the math was simple — *should* have been simple. Just as the battle should have been over in minutes. But these guys were good. Almost too good.

Han half rolled the X-wing and spun it into a descending half loop, reversing direction and speeding after the two freighters on Luke's tail. Their flight paths crisscrossed back and forth, trapping Luke between them. Evading one put him in firing range of the other. They'd caught him in a web, and it was tightening around him.

Han dived into the center of the formation, hurtling toward one of the freighters. It held to its flight path until the last moment and peeled away just before a collision — passing so close that Han caught a glimpse of the pilot's lizard-like snout.

"Thanks for the assist, Red Two," Luke said into the comm.

"Anytime," Han shot back. "Like . . . right about now!" He fired off two blasts at the Preybird, zooming in from four o'clock, laser cannons blazing.

Han couldn't shake the feeling that something wasn't right about this attack. He couldn't put his finger on it, but something was *off* about the way these pilots were targeting them. If he could just take a moment to *think*. . . .

"Red Two, bird on your tail, six o'clock!" Wedge shouted into the comm.

Han dropped altitude abruptly. Laser bolts screamed overhead. Fire strafed his wings. The Preybird was back. Han accelerated, forcing all power to his thrusters, then whipped the ship around and spiraled through a series of gut-churning turns. The Preybird clung to him every step of the way. A burst of fire streaked toward him. Han jerked the ship to the side, forgetting for one fatal moment that this wasn't the *Falcon,* with its temperamental thrusters. He overcompensated, shooting hard to starboard, directly into the firing path of the Firespray.

The laser bolt scored a direct hit on the aft engine. Flames sparked from Han's control panel, and smoke filled the cockpit.

The Firespray closed in for the kill.

Luke slammed the Firespray with a barrage of laserfire. The ship seemed, incredibly, to dance between the bolts, emerging unscathed. But at least it backed off of Han.

"Han, what's your status?" Luke asked, watching anxiously as smoke poured from his friend's X-wing.

There was no answer.

"Han!" Luke shouted, beginning to panic. *"Report!"*

There was another long silence. Then: "Mild damage to aft engine, but it's under control. Thanks for the save, Red Leader."

Luke breathed a thin sigh of relief.

This wasn't working. The enemy might have been outnumbered, but it wasn't stopping them from putting up a fight. This mission was too important to abandon — but Luke refused to lose a member of his squad to this faceless enemy. They needed a new plan—quickly.

He needed a new plan. After all, Commander Narra had put him in charge.

I don't know why, he thought, dispirited.

But it didn't matter if Narra had made a mistake. Luke was in charge, which meant it was his responsibility to guide his men down to the surface. To keep them alive.

"Red Three, Red Four, hold present course," he ordered finally. "Red Two, Red Five, you're with me." The enemy pilots were too formidable as a unit. But divide and conquer — that could work. Wedge and Zev would stay in a high orbit while Luke, Han, and Chewbacca would head for the planet. The enemy would be forced to split up. Three on two was a greater advantage than five on four. And once Luke and the others had dispatched their attackers, they could return to help Wedge and Zev clean up the rest.

It was the perfect plan — except for one thing. As Luke, Han, and Chewbacca dived toward Kamino, the enemy ships *didn't* split up. They stuck close to Luke's trail. Too close.

The Preybird opened fire, followed by the Firespray. And their blasts were concentrated on Luke.

"Reverse course!" he shouted as Kamino loomed in his viewscreen and all four enemy ships strafed him with laserfire. Han and Chewbacca were trying to hold them off, but the three of them were outnumbered. Luke pulled up hard on his controls, attempting to gain altitude and return to Wedge and Zev. But the thrusters wouldn't respond.

It didn't make sense. "Artoo!" he shouted, banking sharply to avoid a blast of fire. He could force the ship into a pitch and roll, but the thrusters weren't giving him any lift. Once the enemy figured out he couldn't shift direction, he'd be toast. "What's going on with the navigational thrusters? Have we been hit?"

R2-D2 beeped something that indicated a negative. He swiveled his domed head and extended a manipulator arm, searching for broken connections. Luke blasted laserfire at the nearest freighter. His targeting and weapons systems were still operational. But the ship was accelerating toward the planet — and there was nothing he could do to stop it.

The strange gravitational readings! Luke suddenly realized. They hadn't been caused by a natural anomaly after all. Some kind of tractor beam had to be dragging his ship toward the planet. "This is Red Leader!" he cried into the comm, panicking. "Retreat! Repeat: Retreat. Something's pulling me toward the planet. All units retreat while there's still time!"

"Time's up, kid," Han said into his comm. "Whatever it is, it's caught me, too." His X-wing went flying past Luke's, with Chewie's close behind. The enemy ships were falling, too. The blasts of laserfire broke off as the pilots tried desperately to pull their ships out of the tractor field.

But nothing Luke did seemed to help. R2-D2 had no luck, either. They were falling, with no way to slow the descent. "If we come in too steep, we'll burn up in the atmosphere!" Luke said, alarmed. But they could only wait — and hope. If he made it through the atmosphere intact, he could eject. If not . . .

"At least Leia's not here," Luke murmured. "That's something."

The deep black of space gave way to the swirling storm clouds of Kamino. The wind screamed past as Luke's X-wing hurtled toward the surface. Wide, flat platforms raised on stilts stretched over a dark, churning sea. The ship would either slam into one of the city platforms and break into a million pieces, or it would drop into the waves and disappear forever. Luke didn't plan to stick around to find out which. He scrounged behind his seat for his survival kit and stuffed it into his utility pouch. It was now or never.

"You ready, little guy?" he asked R2-D2.

The astromech droid beeped encouragingly. Luke took a deep breath — and ejected.

The wind roared in his ears, a deafening thunder. His stomach lurched into his throat. The ground sped toward him; the icy air sliced his face, stole his breath, burned his eyes. Then the parachute deployed.

And all was calm; all was silent.

Luke floated, the wind now nothing but a gentle breeze. The city gradually grew beneath him, spindly gray buildings sprouting from the water, connected by wide, flat platforms. Beyond them, nothing but open sea. In the distance, ships screamed through the sky and crashed into the waves, one after another. *Han and Chewie must have ejected, too,* Luke thought, watching their X-wings disappear beneath the sea. *They* had *to.*

He was able to angle his descent enough to aim for one of the platforms, but at the last minute, a gust of wind blew him off course. The parachute wrapped itself around a long, thin antenna shooting up from the surface. Luke stopped with a jolt as the parachute lines were stretched taut. He found himself dangling upside down, about twenty meters off the ground. Rain pelted his face. Bolts of lightning flashed overhead, dangerously close. It suddenly occurred to him: What if this wasn't an antenna?

What if it was a lightning rod?

Trying not to panic, Luke yanked on the cords holding him to the parachute. He hauled himself upright. *If I can cut myself free, I can climb down the antenna,* he told himself.

As long as he didn't lose his grip.

As long as the wet durasteel surface wasn't so slick he slid to his death.

And as long as he wasn't struck by lightning on the way down.

He had to swing close enough to the antenna to grab hold. He dangled from the ropes, shifting his weight in one direction, then the other. At first he just swayed gently, but soon he was swinging like a pendulum. He slammed into the antenna and wrapped his arms around the wet durasteel. It was so cold that he could already feel his fingers going numb. He'd have to do this fast. Wrapping his legs tightly around the narrow pole, he activated his lightsaber. The glowing blue blade sliced through the parachute cords. Luke was free. Now he just needed to find a way down.

He peered at the ground, which seemed extremely far away. There were no handholds on the antenna, and the material was too slippery to risk climbing hand over hand. Instead, he shinnied down, finding purchase with his feet, then lowering his weight, inch by slippery inch. His hair was plastered to his face and rain streamed into his eyes, turning the world into a watery blur. His hands slipped down the pole with a blistering squeal, and he dropped the last three meters, landing on the ground with a heavy, jolting thud.

But at least he'd made it onto the planet. Now, the next problem: How was he ever going to leave it — especially with his ship at the bottom of the Kamino sea?

The city, a collection of dark domed buildings rising on stilts from the choppy waters, was absolutely still. According to Luke's mission briefing, the place was little more than barracks for the families of those working in the research station, so it made sense that much of the population would have left when the station had closed down. He'd been expecting a sparse population, a certain emptiness, but he hadn't expected . . . *this.*

The platforms were empty. Motionless. And yet signs of life were everywhere. Speeders sat in the middle of the street, apparently abandoned, rusting in the rain. Peering through water-streaked windows, Luke glimpsed homes with tables set for dining, offices with work-cluttered desks, children's playrooms strewn with toys. It was as if one day all the residents had simultaneously dropped what they were doing and walked away.

Or disappeared.

There was a rustling noise behind him. Luke froze. He rested his hand on his blaster and slowly turned around.

R2-D2 beeped in delight. Luke relaxed and smiled in relief. "Glad you made it, little guy. Now we just have to find the others." He pulled out his survival pack. It was equipped with a homing beacon and a signal detector that would allow him to track the beacons of the other X-wing pilots. Two blinking lights popped up on the screen — one for Han, one for Chewbacca. They were close — less than a kilometer away. The signal tracker would show him exactly where to find his friends. But it couldn't tell him whether they were still alive.

Div turned his back on his ship before it sank completely beneath the water. No point in dwelling on the past — and his beloved Firespray was now officially *past*. When the tractor beam had first kicked in, he had assumed it was part of Skywalker's attack. But it quickly became clear that the Rebel X-wings were just as helpless as Div and his pilots — which meant the beam was coming from the planet. *Probably some kind of Imperial defense system,* Div thought. His employer had promised that this sector of Kamino was abandoned. But Imperial defenses were sophisticated; they didn't need human personnel to operate them. No doubt this one had been left activated when the scientists had fled. Div would need to go to the central research station, deactivate the beam, and find a ship that would take him off this rock. The sooner he was back in the air, the sooner he could complete his mission. That is, if Skywalker hadn't died on impact.

He's alive, Div thought. *Out there somewhere. Close.*

Logic dictated that if Div had had time to eject, Skywalker and his friends probably had, too. But it wasn't logic that made him so sure. Sometimes Div just knew things. And he knew that Luke Skywalker was alive.

Not for long, friend, Div thought. When he agreed to take a job, he never stopped until he got it done.

It soon became clear that the city had been completely abandoned. The briefing files from his employer had included all known information about Kamino, but that wasn't saying much. Nearly all the data had focused on Tipoca City and its satellite communities. It was there, in the planet's capital, that the Republic's clone warriors had been born.

No, not born. *Made.*

Built.

Div suppressed a shudder, thinking of the blank, identical expressions lying beneath those blinding white hoods. He'd been only a young child when the Republic fell and the clones became Imperial weapons of terror.

But he couldn't understand how anyone had been foolish enough to trust them, to see them as protectors. As anything but the face of a pitiless and indomitable enemy.

Because they were fools, Div reminded himself. Quick to trust; quick to die. He knew better that than most.

The images of Tipoca City in his briefing files showed a vast network of huge domed towers. Kamino's capital was nearly entirely enclosed and protected from the elements, its scientists moving through immaculate white halls, their lives showered in light.

But *this* city . . . well, you could hardly call it a city at all. *Research City,* the briefing file had deemed it, offering no images—only a map and blueprints of the central research station. It was dark where Tipoca City was light, corroded with mud and grime and rust where Tipoca City was spotlessly clean. While most of the buildings were domed, in the style of Kaminoan architecture, the network of hatchways connecting them was incomplete. Div suspected that the Empire had never planned for full enclosure. It may have been the traditional Kamino way, but it was also costly and timely. This city—or outpost, really—showed all the signs of something of built in a hurry. Or half-built, at least. There were abandoned construction sites on every corner, as if the workers had left in the middle of the job. *As if they left in a hurry,* Div thought. And so the city had been left open to the elements. With no one left to care for them, the buildings were already corroding in the steady rain. Div wondered how long it would take for the lightning rods atop each dome to topple. For the domes to collapse in on themselves. For the stilts holding up the city platforms to fail. For the city to be fully reclaimed by the sea.

By that time, he planned to be long gone.

Div sloshed through rain-flooded gutters, wandering aimlessly — or so it would have seemed to anyone watching. But he had memorized a map of the city and was following a meandering path to the central research station. It was the likeliest place to find a ship. Div had learned a long time ago that a strange environment was a dangerous one. He had to find his bearings and explore the surroundings before walking blindly into what could be a trap.

Something else Div had learned long ago: Anything could be a trap.

The storm clouds cast the city in permanent shadow. Div knew that Kaminoans saw only in ultraviolet, so to them, the buildings likely shimmered in an array of colors invisible to the human eye. But to him, the city was nothing but a bleak landscape of black and white. Thunder rumbled gently in the distance, blending with the rhythmic slapping of the surf and — something else.

Div froze midstep. The telltale click of the blaster was almost too soft to hear, but it was unmistakable.

He whirled around, weapon raised, and came face to face with a blaster carbine.

"Div, right? My *leader*?" The woman holding the rifle was one of the pilots on his team, a hard-edged mercenary who'd said no more than two or three words to anyone. Clea Sook, he remembered. From Galidraan. It'd be hard to forget the black tattoos covering her face and hands — hands that were aiming a blaster at his head, without trembling. Div was pretty sure she could easily shoot him and never look back. "Any good orders you'd like to hand out now?"

"How about: Drop the blaster?" Div said, without much hope it would have an effect. "We could work together, find our way out of here twice as fast."

Clea's lips curled up in a mirthless smile.

"You really don't want to aim that at me," Div added.

"Let's see. . . . With you alive, I split the reward four ways. With you dead, I split it three ways. Why *wouldn't* I want to aim this at you?" She laughed. "You think I can't survive on this rock without your help?"

"Maybe you can; maybe you can't," Div allowed. "But there's one thing you won't survive."

"What's that?"

"This." He struck out before she had a chance to react. His arm slashed across hers in a blur of motion. The blaster flew from her hand. In seconds, he had her on the ground, his knee on her chest, his blaster jabbing her forehead. Div tilted his head. "You sure you don't want to reconsider working together?"

She scowled at him. "Why not just kill me now, up your share of the reward?"

"Because no one's getting anything until we blast off this planet," Div said. "Besides . . ." Without taking his attention off her, he widened his focus to include the cityscape. It was perfectly still and silent. No signs of life. And yet he couldn't shake the feeling that something was out there. Something *wrong*. "Besides, no point in working alone when we can work together."

"And if I don't agree to buddy up?" she asked flatly, clearly already knowing the answer.

"Leave you out here, knowing you want me dead?" he asked. "Would *you* do that?"

Clea smiled, genuinely this time. "Not if I wanted to live." She nodded. "Fine. We work together." She raised a hand, and he shook it, then pulled her to her feet. He was pretty sure she'd strike the moment his back was turned. So he returned her blaster, but not before deactivating it with a subtle, practiced motion. She'd never know, unless she tried to shoot.

Div let Clea lead the way to the research station, devoting most of his attention to the dark corners of the silent city. Her reflexes were slow, her motions obvious.

Her face was a transparent mask that announced her every impulse as soon as she had it. She was a known quantity, and that meant she wasn't a threat.

It was the unknown that bothered him. Not *scared* him, not yet. But something was out there, in the shadows flickering in the abandoned streets. *Come and get me,* Div thought. *I'll be ready.* He always was.

Almost *always,* he thought bitterly, brushing away the memory as soon as it arose. He'd let his guard down one time and someone else had paid the price. It wasn't going to happen again.

Ever.

Fallon Pollo lurched down the narrow street, blood seeping from a gash in his leg. All his equipment — his food, comlink, weapons, map — had gone down with his ship. He had crashed at the edge of the city, his Preybird smashing through the roof of an abandoned barracks. The driving rains had blotted out the fire, and Fallon had escaped. No amount of money was worth this kind of grief. But then, he didn't fly for money, did he? Not anymore. All his life, he'd chased the big score, the one last job that would let him retire in style.

The job had taken ten years to find, two months to complete.

Retirement had lasted about two weeks.

So he was back in the game, picking and choosing jobs at random. He had a reputation for being particular, turning down high-paying gigs for no apparent reason. The truth was he didn't have a reason for anything he did, not anymore. He worked until he became bored, then took a break — and when he was bored with playing, he worked again. He had everything a man could want: money, luxury, freedom. Now he wanted nothing, except an escape from the boredom.

And that was harder and harder to find.

He trudged aimlessly, searching for a sign of life. He kept his eyes on the ground, ignoring the gray buildings looming overhead.

Ignoring the dark shadow that trailed him, and the soft, wet slurping sounds it made as it slithered down the street.

Fallon rounded a corner, finding himself in a dark, narrow alley. It dead-ended after a few feet, abruptly dropping off into the water. Fallon hesitated at the edge, staring down at the roiling seas. Bolts of lightning danced at the horizon. Heavy clouds cast the world in permanent night. A few aiwhas, flying lizards with ten-meter wingspans, circled low on the water, searching for food. They suddenly scattered, as if spooked by his presence, and disappeared over the horizon. Fallon was wholly alone.

Thunder crashed and wind whipped across the water. Through the noise of the rising storm, Fallon couldn't hear the quiet slap of tentacles lashing the pavement.

But something made him turn around.

His face went pale. His mouth dropped open. Eyes pinned on the nightmare before him, he grasped stupidly for his blaster. Just as his hand closed around the trigger, a giant maw opened before him and the darkness swallowed him whole.

Fallon Pollo was no more. Yet the creature was still hungry — and the night was alive with fresh prey.

CHAPTER FIVE

What do you mean you have a bad feeling about this?" Han growled. "Quit messing around, you oversized hairball, and let's go find Luke."

Chewbacca looked nervously at the deserted streets and barked a quiet reply.

"I don't *know* where everyone went," Han said. "So how about we figure out a way off the planet, before they come back?"

Shrugging his massive shoulders, Chewbacca lumbered alongside Han as they followed the tracking beacon in hopes it would lead them to Luke. Han choked back a laugh, knowing that it was never a good idea to laugh at a Wookiee, even when he was your copilot and best friend. Still, he couldn't help but chuckle over the fact that Chewbacca, who stood more than two meters tall and could crush a man's throat in his mighty fist, was afraid of a few empty buildings.

He had to admit, the quiet was kind of creepy. Commander Narra had told them that the research station was abandoned; he hadn't mentioned that an entire city had gone with it. What could have made all those people just drop everything and walk away?

Maybe they didn't walk, Han thought, staring at an overturned speeder lying in the middle of the road. *Maybe they ran.*

Han shook his head. Now he was thinking like Chewie. Han wasn't about to let this place spook him. He had better things to do.

He and Chewbacca had landed within half a kilometer of one another. Once they'd found each other, they'd tried raising Luke on the comlink. No luck. Similar silence from Wedge and Zev. He hoped they were still up in orbit, planning a rescue. But Han wasn't willing to count on it. For all he knew, they'd given the rest of Red Squadron up for dead and headed back to Yavin 4. Or another formation of enemy pilots had blown them out of the sky. No, he didn't plan on waiting around here for rescue. He and Chewbacca and Luke would find a way out of this place themselves.

Assuming Luke was still alive.

According to the beacon, they were approaching his location. "Luke!" Han shouted, his voice echoing through the empty streets. "Hello! Anyone there? Luke!"

Chewbacca tried to quiet him, but Han shook off the Wookiee. They should be practically on top of Luke, so where was he?

He heard a quiet rustling sound behind him. He whirled around. "Luke? Where have you—*aaaaah!*" A giant lizard, its gray-green wings stretching nearly ten meters across, swooped low over Han. His coat snagged on the creature's ragged harness, and before he knew it, his feet had left the ground. "Hey! Hey, let me go, you overgrown mynock."

The creature swooped into the air, wheeling in circles through the clouds. Han scrabbled for his blaster and aimed it at the beast's underbelly—but didn't pull the trigger. The ground was shrinking beneath him, and killing the creature now would lead to both of them plunging to their deaths.

See, Highness? he thought wryly. *I don't* always *shoot before I think.*

Han had heard about aiwhas, the giant winged cetaceans that ruled the seas and skies of Kamino. But hearing was different from *seeing.* The creature was enormous, covered with a thick, scaly hide. It was hard to believe that such a great beast could ever have been domesticted. But it surely had been—its riding harness was still in place, if a little worse for wear. The aiwha let loose a stream of ear-piercing screeches, and Han spotted several winged shadows emerging from the clouds, heeding its call.

Just fly a little closer to the ground, Han thought, *and I've got a little surprise for you.* As if obeying his silent command, the giant winged creature streaked toward the ground, chasing after two of its scaly friends. The aiwha in the lead let out a piercing shriek as Chewbacca sent a bolt of laserfire into its shoulder. It flapped furiously, its right wing smacking the other aiwha off course.

Startled, the aiwha holding Han ascended sharply, fleeing the blaster. "Wrong way, lizard breath!" Han shouted. But it was no use. The aiwha rose higher and higher.

Just then Luke stepped out of the shadows, his light-saber extended over his head. "Come and get me!" he shouted at the aiwha. The blue blade slashed back and forth, a single spot of light in the dim, murky air.

That's it, Han thought as the aiwha streaked toward Luke. *Just a little closer to the ground and — now!* He aimed the blaster at the aiwha's underbelly.

"No!" Luke shouted. "Han, don't —"

Han squeezed the trigger as he tore at his jacket. A stream of laserfire sizzled into the aiwha, bouncing off its leathery skin. It howled in rage and pain, ascending steeply. But Han couldn't work himself loose. "Come on, birdbrain," he growled, pounding his blaster against the buckle. "Let me *go!*"

The jacket tore. Han plummeted through the air and crashed into something soft and scratchy. It smelled like moldy muja fruit. The aiwha, still screeching and flailing from its wound, swooped toward him again. Han held it off with the blaster, trying to figure out where he'd ended up. He was in a hollow dish-shaped space made of grass and seaweed. Three large gray spheres were tucked beneath some of the seaweed.

Uh-oh, Han thought, suddenly realizing where he was. Those weren't spheres. They were *eggs*.

He was in the aiwha's nest.

Luke peered up. Way up. The nest was wedged into the roof of one of the enormous domed buildings. The creatures seemed to be afraid of Han's blaster, so he was having no trouble holding them off. But there were no obvious footholds in the sloping roof, no way for Han to climb down safely. And even if there had been, it would have meant turning his back on the creatures. Luke was pretty sure that the moment that happened, they would strike.

If Han couldn't descend by himself, Luke was going to have to rescue him. "Cover me," he told Chewbacca. The Wookiee didn't need an invitation. He hoisted his bowcaster and sprayed the skies with energy bolts. R2-D2 wheeled in circles around him, beeping and whirring in distress.

"I'm coming, Han!" Luke shouted, carving two narrow crevices into the wall with his lightsaber. He figured he could continue carving handholds and footholds for himself as he scaled his way up to the roof.

"Don't bother," Han shouted down. "I'll figure something out."

"What?" Luke called.

There was a long pause. Luke continued carving and climbing, painfully dragging himself up along the slick durasteel.

"I'm working on it!" Han finally shouted, blasting at an aiwha who'd foolishly drawn too close.

Luke would have laughed, but he needed all his energy to hold his weight. Finally, he made it to the top and pulled himself into the nest.

"I *told* you I didn't need your help," Han said, scowling. "Now we're both stuck up here. What good does that do?"

"This, for one thing," Luke said, pulling out his blaster and adding to Han's attack. The aiwhas shrieked and cawed, their wings beating furiously.

"They're never going to abandon the nest!" Han said. "We have to get down from here."

"That's the plan," Luke answered. "After you. I'll hold them off."

"After *you*, kid," Han insisted. The skies darkened as a thick cloud blew their way.

Far below, Chewbacca roared impatiently.

Luke's eyes widened. That was no cloud. It was a flock of aiwhas, at least twenty of them, coming straight for the nest. "How about we both go!" he said, pointing toward the flock. *"Now."*

They dived out of the nest and scrambled down the side of the building toward Chewbacca, clinging tightly to the niches carved out by the lightsaber. The aiwhas tore after them, their massive wings beating in a rhythmic thunder. Han, Luke, and Chewbacca ran through the empty streets, over permacrete gleaming in the rain, feet sloshing through puddles as they fled from the aiwhas. Soon they'd left the thunder of the wings far behind. The night was still again, silence broken only by the rumbling thunder and the distant waves.

"You're welcome," Han said once they'd all caught their breath.

"I'm welcome?" Luke asked incredulously. "For what?"

"We found you, didn't we?" Han said. "If we hadn't come looking for you, you'd be wandering around on your own. You would've made a nice, tasty dinner for some baby birds."

"Aiwhas are herbivores," Luke pointed out. "And I found *you.* If it weren't for me, you'd still be up in that nest, waiting to hatch."

Chewbacca growled his agreement.

"Aw, can it, furball," Han snapped. "At least I'm not afraid of the dark."

Luke was tempted to keep arguing, but they had bigger problems to deal with. "Have you had any luck contacting Wedge or Zev?" Luke asked.

Han shook his head. "They must have been too far from the planet's surface. Weren't caught in the beam."

Unlike us, Luke thought, flushing. It was his fault they were trapped here. *He* had been in charge of the mission, and he was the one who'd ordered that final maneuver, bringing the three of them closer to the planet's surface. If one of them hadn't made it, there would have been no one to blame but himself.

"Hey, kid, don't beat yourself up about it," Han said, as if he knew what Luke was thinking. He clapped him on the shoulder. "None of us knew about that tractor beam. You couldn't have guessed—"

"But I knew *something* was off," Luke insisted. "I should have . . ." He shook his head. He didn't know what the right choice had been, only that he'd made the wrong one. "I should have been more careful."

"A firefight's no place for careful," Han said. "And it's no place for what-ifs. You made the call you had to make, *in that moment.* It was a good maneuver; I would have done the same. And you might have saved all our lives."

"How do you figure that?" Luke asked, a little sourly.

"What if we'd won that fight, blasted all those ships out of the sky?" Han said. "We'd have come in for a landing, and we'd all have been caught in the beam. At least this way Wedge and Zev are still out there some-where — hopefully coming up with a plan."

"We can't count on that," Luke said.

"You're right. And even if they are out there, they can't do anything until we shut down that tractor beam."

"It must be an old security system, left behind by the Empire," Luke said. "We've have to find it. Then, *if* we can disable it —"

R2-D2 beeped indignantly.

"Okay, okay." Luke patted R2-D2's dome. "*When* we disable it, maybe we'll be able to find a ship."

"And it'd be handy if we arrived before the others," Han added. "So let's go."

"Others?" Luke asked. "You think those pilots sur-vived the crash?"

"We did," Han pointed out.

Luke glanced over his shoulder, suddenly feeling like someone was watching them. The city was absolutely still. Nothing was out there but the rain — for now.

They decided to start by finding the research sta-tion. If there was an Imperial security system, or even a fleet of Imperial ships, that seemed the best place to find it.

The base was a low complex of black windowless domes nearly three times the size of the other buildings they'd passed. Luke had expected that they'd have to break in, but the central doors were wide open. Chewbacca growled.

"Yeah," Han agreed. "It is strange. But they want company? I'm not arguing." He pulled out his blaster and stepped inside. Luke followed close behind, lightsaber in hand. The blade cast an eerie blue glow over the station. Despite its size, the low ceilings gave it a claustrophobic feel, as if the curved walls were closing in on them. The entry corridor opened into a wide atrium space dotted with personal lab stations. Cages lined its perimeter, all of them empty. One quadrant of the room was given over to a large pool of water. As Luke approached, he realized that the scientists had merely opened a hole in the floor; he was peering down into the Kaminoan sea.

Turning his back on the water, Luke hesitated. He didn't like this. The wide space was completely open. And he couldn't shake the feeling that someone was watching.

"Come on," Han whispered harshly. "What are you waiting for?"

"I'm not sure," Luke said, raking his gaze across the empty station.

"There's no one here."

"Then why are you whispering?" Luke asked.

"I said, there's *no one here*," Han repeated loudly.

"Then who are we?" a voice behind them asked. Luke pivoted, blaster raised, and found himself face to face with a blaster muzzle. The man pointing the weapon was tall and thin, with an angular face covered in brown scruff. He was flanked by a sharp-toothed Chistori in full body armor and an angry-looking woman with tattoos inked across her face. Their blasters were trained on Luke, Han, and Chewbacca.

Han's blaster was armed and aimed at the Chistori's head. Chewbacca issued a low warning growl. The woman took a step back, but her blaster never wavered.

"So what now?" Luke murmured, catching Han's eye.

The woman heard him. Her lips widened into an ice-cold smile. "Now? Now you die."

lea, stand down!" Div snapped. "You, too, Grish."

The Chistori gave him a surly look. He drew back his lips to reveal a mouthful of jagged teeth. "I don't think so."

Div had seen pictures of Luke Skywalker. The Rebel had looked the same in all of them — wide-eyed, slightly dazed, clueless, and young. The man standing before him, blaster aimed, wore the same face. But he was older, angrier. That open, trusting look in his eyes was gone.

"Do me a favor, keep your blasters up," said the one called Han Solo. "It'll make the target practice more fun."

The Wookiee just growled.

Div sighed. "Don't be an idiot," he said, speaking to both Grish and Solo. Hotheads, both of them. If the situation wasn't under control soon, they'd probably blow each other away — and everyone else along with them. He and Clea had stumbled upon Grish shortly after teaming up — but Div couldn't help wondering if they would have been better off without the Chistori's so-called help. "We're no threat to you," he assured the Rebels.

Han laughed. "Tell me something I don't know."

"We have no wish to harm you," Div clarified. "So you can drop the weapons."

"You tried to blow us out of the sky!" Luke exclaimed.

"Kid's got a point," Han said. "Sounds like harm to me."

Without taking his eyes off the Rebels, Div surveyed the room, weighing the possibilities. There were only two exit points — the way they'd come in, and another corridor feeding off the opposite side of the room, leading deeper into the station. The odd pool of water lay between them, a narrow bridge offering a way across. The bridge would be a less-than-defensible position should things go bad. The lab stations would provide minimal cover, although several of them featured low durasteel cabinets that looked large enough to hold a human. But hiding wasn't really his style.

A flicker of movement along the water caught his attention. But nothing was there. *Trick of the light,* he told himself. *Must have been.* But he wasn't convinced. "We all want off this planet," Div said, feeling a sudden urgency. "Let's make that a priority, and deal with this —"

"*This?*" Luke said angrily. "That's what you call it? You attack us for no reason, you make us crash —"

"Hey, slimesuckers like that couldn't 'make' me do anything," Han protested.

"*Riiiight,*" Clea drawled. "You *wanted* to crash-land on this moldy rock."

"No more or less than you, sweetheart," Han said.

She narrowed her eyes, and her grip tightened around the blaster.

"Clea," Div said quietly. She didn't acknowledge him. But she didn't shoot, either.

"What the shunfa are we waiting for?" Grish growled. "I say we blast this scum. There's a reward waiting for us. Just because we're stuck here, no reason not to get the job done."

"Enough!" Div snapped.

But it was too late. "Reward?" Luke said. "So someone hired you to come after us?"

"Jabba," Solo muttered in disgust. "I *told* him he'd have his money soon. Why can't that fat slug just trust me?"

But Div could see that Luke wasn't convinced. "Who was it?" Luke asked Div. "Who wants us dead?"

"That's not your concern," Div told him.

"Then let's start with an easier question," Han said. "Who are *you*?"

Div shrugged. "What's the difference? All that matters is that we have a job to do. A job that requires us to be in the *air*," he reminded his allies. "We're pilots, not bounty hunters. Not *assassins*. We don't stalk our prey on foot and shoot them in the back. We're better than that. I say we work together. Once we're back in space, we do what we were hired to do — best them in a firefight. *Up there,* where we belong."

"You think we're some kind of laserbrained nerf-herders?" Han asked. "I put this blaster down, what's to stop you from shooting the minute I turn my back?"

"I don't know if you're a laserbrained nerf-herder," Div said, although he had his suspicions. "But I give you my word that we won't harm you, not until we're all back in the air."

"Your word?" Han's mouth puckered. "What good does that do any of us?"

Not much, Div was about to admit, realizing that this was a losing battle. He had nothing to bargain with but his words, and they'd never been worth much. But before he could speak, he spotted Luke's glance flicker toward something on the other side of the room — the same place Div had imagined he'd spotted a shadow in motion. Div followed Luke's gaze and saw nothing. But Luke's face was draining of color. He leaned toward Solo and whispered something, but the older man shrugged him off. Div searched in frustration for some sign of what had made the Rebel turn gray with fear, but there was nothing. It was as if Luke were in a different room, a different world than the rest of them. *What does he know that I don't?* Div thought.

Something was naggingly familiar about the way the young Rebel stood, visibly extending the reach of his senses as far as he could, opening himself up to the room. His eyes narrowed and turned toward the pool of black water.

What? Div thought, his stomach twisting with sudden anxiety. *What is it about you? What do you see?*

The cold pressure of alloy against his temple snapped his attention back to matters at hand, but it was too late.

"The nerf-herder's right," Clea snarled, her blaster muzzle digging into his forehead. "They have no reason to trust you. And neither do we."

Div cursed under his breath. It wasn't like him, letting an enemy sneak up on him like that. What good were his lightning reflexes and impeccable instincts if he was going to let himself be so easily distracted? "There's no need for this," he told Clea.

"Either you join us, or you die with them," Clea said. "And you die first."

Div turned to the Chistori, without much hope. "Grish —"

"Choose, human," Grish said. "Or we choose for you."

Div knew he could disarm Clea and probably Grish before either of them got off a shot. But it would leave them all vulnerable to an attack by the Rebels. He couldn't take on all five by himself.

He'd meant what he'd said: He was a pilot, not a bounty hunter. He'd been hired to best Skywalker from the cockpit. But he wasn't about to sacrifice his life for a bunch of strangers. *No difference between shooting them here and shooting them up there,* he told himself.

"Han, it's coming," Luke said suddenly, sounding alarmed.

"Kid, not now, we're —"

"No. *Now!*" Luke cried, pointing at something behind Div. "Run!"

Grish issued a harsh chuckle. "You think I'm going to fall for that one? Maybe *you* die first, for treating me like a koochu." A flash of green laserfire streamed from his blaster, but Luke was already in motion, diving for cover. Solo and the Wookiee raced after Luke.

"Behind you, Grish," Div said quietly, slowly inching backward. Out of the corner of his eye, he saw Clea run. Probably the smarter move. But Div stood his ground.

"If I'm not going to buy it from him, why would I buy it from *you*? You think — *blaaaaghraugh!*" The noise he made was a combination of a gurgle, a scream, and a snort as a long, thick tentacle wrapped around his chest. His blaster clattered to the floor.

The . . . *thing* hoisted Grish off the ground. It was at least six meters tall, with black skin that shimmered like an oil slick. Its mouth, a gaping maw rimmed with jagged teeth, was nearly as wide as its torso. It moved with surprising speed, dragging itself on six thick, powerful tentacles. And at the tip of each tentacle, a razor-sharp retractable claw sprouted. Div's blaster shots bounced off the beast's scaly hide. The creature issued a keening moan but never loosened its grip on Grish. Then the beast opened its massive jaws and swallowed the Chistori whole.

CHAPTER SEVEN

The pilots scattered. Han dived for cover beneath a storage bin. Chewbacca pried loose a strip of wall paneling and wedged himself into a crevice, shielding himself with the strip of thick transparisteel. Luke ducked behind one of the lab stations. He peered through a crack in the durasteel, watching the creature slime across the laboratory. For a beast of its size, it moved remarkably fast.

Instead of hiding, the enemy pilots ran, even though the beast stood between them and the exit. The creature was too fast for them. It cut them off and lunged toward the woman, its jaw gaping wide. She fired her blaster, but the laserfire just glanced off its scaly chest.

"No!" the other pilot shouted, raking blasterfire up and down the beast's body, searching for a weak spot. Nothing penetrated the hide or even slowed the creature down. It pounced again. The woman darted out of the way just in time, but the creature swung at her with one of its thick tentacles and knocked her off her feet.

Luke couldn't just stand by and watch. Even if she'd been trying to kill him a few moments before, she didn't deserve to die like this. No one did. He jumped up from behind the lab station and shot his blaster at the ceiling. "Over here!"

"What do you think you're doing?" Han whispered fiercely from his hiding space.

Luke ignored Han — and the creature ignored Luke, who rushed to help the pilots. But before he could reach them, the woman let loose a bloodcurdling scream. And she was gone.

There was no time to panic or mourn. The creature was still hungry. Luke joined the other pilot. The beast looked even larger close up. It loomed over them, at least three times their size. Luke sprayed it with blasterfire, searching for a stretch of skin that wasn't covered by leathery armored hide. But the monster's flesh seemed impenetrable. Their combined blasterfire was holding the creature at bay, but just barely. The distance between them narrowed.

Suddenly, there was a loud crack, and a chunk of duracrete exploded from the ceiling, crashing down on the creature's head. It spasmed in pain and jerked out of the way, revealing Han and Chewbacca standing behind it, their weapons aimed at the ceiling. "What are you staring at, kid?" Han shouted. "Let's blast this thing back where it came from!"

Luke began firing again, this time aiming for the monster's gaping mouth, in hopes that it would be more sensitive than the rest of the creature's body. Luke's laser-fire strafed the creature's thick black tongue, and it began to shriek with pain. Driven backward by the combined firepower of four blasters, wounded and in pain, the creature lashed a long tentacle at Han and Chewbacca, knocking them off their feet. "Han!" Luke cried in alarm.

But the creature didn't move in for the kill. Instead, having cleared a path for itself, it slithered swiftly across the room and plunged into the large pool of water with a noisy splash. It disappeared beneath the surface, leaving nothing behind but rippling water and a trail of blood.

Div stared at the spot where Clea had lain waiting for the creature to strike. At the last moment, she'd stopped fighting back; she'd given up. He had seen it in her eyes: the dull, hopeless look of a cornered animal just waiting to die.

That will never be me, he told himself. He'd seen too much death to give himself up to it willingly. Fight to the last breath — that was the only way to stay alive.

Someone tapped his shoulder, and he flinched, instinctively swiveling his blaster toward the nearest target. Luke Skywalker.

"I said, are you all right?" Luke asked.

The other one, Han Solo, said nothing. But he kept his blaster aimed steadily at Div's head. The Wookiee stood by his side, growling warily.

"Fine," Div said shortly. He didn't like standing out in the open like this. The creature could be back at any moment. And it didn't give him much comfort that the combined strength of three blasters had done little more than irritate its hide.

"I guess now we know why this place was abandoned," Han said, shaking his head. "What *was* that thing?"

"The latest Imperial *wonder*," Div said darkly. "Aren't we lucky to live in a time of such advanced civilization?"

Luke's eyes widened. "You think the Empire *created* that thing?" he asked.

It had been less than a minute, and Div was already exhausted by the Rebel's breathless naïveté. "Kaminoan scientists employed by the Empire," he said, annoyed by having to explain something so basic. "They're expert genetic manipulators, and obviously that . . . *creature* didn't have natural origins."

Luke and Han exchanged a glance, and Han gave Luke a nearly imperceptible nod. "Surprised you're not more impressed," Han said.

"Impressed? By the Emperor's latest killing machine?" Div raised an eyebrow. "The slaughter of innocent people doesn't impress me, nor the tools used to do it."

"That's surprising coming from someone who turned *himself* into an Imperial killing machine," Luke said angrily.

Div stiffened. "What's that supposed to mean?"

"It means if you hate the Empire so much, why would you work for them?"

"Easy. I wouldn't."

Luke laughed. "Who do you think sent you out here to kill us?"

"None of your business," Div said angrily. "But I assure you it wasn't the Empire."

"Why, because they *told* you so?" Luke's sarcasm was heavy and awkward, and Div could tell it wasn't a tone the Rebel adopted very often.

But the taunt was harder to shrug off than it should have been. Div liked to tell himself that he didn't do business with the Empire. But these days, when you followed money, you often found yourself at the Emperor's doorstep. If it wasn't the Empire, it was Jabba's gang, and if it wasn't Jabba, it was Xizor and the Black Sun syndicate — and when you dug deep enough, there was no real difference between them. They were all bloodthirsty thugs who'd acquired a taste for power. It was true that Div had never knowingly worked for any of them.

But ignorance was easy when you didn't want to know.

What would Trever think? The thought popped into his head without his permission, and he blotted it out just as quickly. He knew exactly what Trever would have thought — that he'd sold out, abandoned his principles, abandoned his people. That he'd given up, just like Clea, and was now just waiting to die.

But Trever was the one who'd died.

The Empire had taken his mother, his stepfather, everyone he'd ever known or cared about. Not to mention Ry-Gaul, Solace, Garen Muln . . . all the names and faces he'd forced himself to forget. And Div had learned his lesson. You did what you needed to do to survive. Even if it meant keeping your head down and your mouth shut.

"How about you lower that blaster?" he suggested to Han.

"How about I put a hole in you before you put one in me?" Han shot back.

"You want to shoot me, shoot me," Div said, thinking, *Good luck with that.* Han's reflexes were fast; that was clear enough. But he was no match for Div. "All I care about is escaping this planet in one piece."

"So you can kill us in space?" Luke said snidely.

Div shrugged. "May the best pilot win, right? But we'll never know who that is until we're back up there. So how about no one blasts anyone until that happens?

Deal?" He lowered his blaster. Someone had to go first.

"I don't make deals with men who try to kill me," Han growled. "It's a quick way to end up dead." But he lowered his blaster, too. He jerked his head at Luke. "Come on, kid. Let's go find ourselves a ship."

Div watched them file out of the laboratory, the tiny astromech droid wheeling dutifully behind. Han paused in the doorway, glaring at Div. "Well?" he drawled. "What are you waiting for?"

Han waited impatiently as R2-D2 probed the research station's computer system. "Take your time," he said sarcastically after several minutes had elapsed. "It's not like we're in any danger."

But the little astromech droid kept working with his manipulator arm plugged into the socket, softly whirring as he sifted through the reams of data. They had concluded that the computer was the best place to start. Rather than wandering randomly through the station, hoping luck would show them the way, they had decided to leave their fate up to R2-D2's data-crunching skills.

At least, *Luke* had decided. When it came to a choice between trusting his gut and trusting a droid, Han chose his gut, each and every time. Even though their mission had gone astray, Luke was still in charge. And Han had to admit that a map would come in handy. *If* the scraphead could find one.

With a triumphant trill of beeps and whistles, R2-D2 drew them over to the computer screen. A detailed schematic of the research station spread across it, two docking bays clearly marked on opposite ends of the building.

"Good job, Artoo!" Luke said, patting the astromech's silver-plated head.

"That's some droid," the enemy pilot said.

Han glared at him. He'd agreed to let the man come along on their search for ships — no doubt an extra blaster could come in handy — but that didn't make them allies. The temporary truce didn't extend to polite small talk.

"Let's go," Han said gruffly. "We'll find ourselves a ship while the droid deals with the security system." A ship would do them no good if they couldn't disable the tractor beam that had dragged them to the surface to begin with.

"You want to leave Artoo *behind*?" Luke asked.

Chewbacca growled his own hesitation at the idea.

Luke shook his head. "I don't —"

"What are you worried about?" Han cut in. They couldn't waste any more time; the longer they stuck around, the shorter their lives were likely to be. "You think that . . . *whatever* you want to call it would eat a rusty bucket of bolts when there's so much fresh meat wandering around? He'll be fine."

"He's probably right," the enemy pilot said. "From what I could tell of the creature, organic-based nutrients seem to be —"

"Let's go," Han said shortly, shooting the pilot a nasty look. As if he needed the man's help to convince Luke of the obvious. "Sooner we go, sooner we can come back for him."

"He's right, you'll be fine," Luke told R2-D2, sounding unconvinced. "You sure you can disable that security system?"

The droid beeped confidently.

Luke still looked worried. "We'll come back for you, Artoo. I promise."

Han cleared his throat. "Enough with the tearful good-byes, kid."

"Let's go," Luke agreed.

They crept down the dark hallways single file. Chewbacca took the lead, his bowcaster in his hands, ready to fire. Han followed him, darting his eyes from side to side, seeking out any dark corner in which a monster might lurk. Luke brought up the rear, keeping his eyes peeled for a threat from behind — or from the mystery pilot, who could turn on them at any moment.

Their footsteps echoed through the empty station. Dim, flickering emergency lights lined the corridor, casting off an eerie glow. Several of the rooms they passed contained large pools of water — some man-made like the one in the atrium, others little more than large jagged gashes in the floor, as if something large and angry had chewed its way through. Han suppressed a shudder and focused on putting one foot in front of the other.

Nothing interrupted the quiet but their footfalls and a rhythmic drip, water droplets spattering to the durasteel floor.

Drip.

Drip.

Drip.

Han looked up suddenly, a drop of water splashing onto his forehead. The water was flowing in small rivulets from large overhead gratings. They likely led to air or heating ducts — but that wouldn't explain where the water was coming from.

Unless . . .

Han froze. "Chewie," he whispered, swiveling his blaster toward the nearest grate, "Luke, do either of you —"

There was a strangled scream behind him. *Div.* Han whirled around — just in time to see the monstrous beast looming over Luke. A busted ceiling grate lay on the floor next to him.

"Look out, kid!" Han shouted, firing at the beast. But he was too late. The jaws were already descending toward Luke. A moment later, they'd swallowed him whole.

"No!" Han screamed. He and Chewbacca unleashed all their firepower on the monstrous creature. It roared and fled from the blasts, slithering up the wall and disappearing into the air ducts.

Han couldn't breathe. It had all happened so fast. One scream, one blur of motion, and then nothing left but the acrid stench of smoke and charred flesh. He squeezed his hands around his blaster, silently urging the beast to return so he could slaughter it.

But the beast was gone.

The enemy pilot was gone.

And Luke —

Han staggered against the wall. Chewbacca moaned.

Luke was gone.

Luke woke up screaming.

He opened his eyes, but the world remained totally dark.

He was trapped somewhere, sealed up tightly against the light. *Either that or I'm blind,* Luke thought, trying to keep the panic at bay. After all, it was a miracle he wasn't dead. Yet. He tried to focus on that.

He couldn't move.

Blind and paralyzed, he thought, struck by a sudden horror. *Maybe I am dead. Maybe this is what death means.*

An eternity, silent and motionless. An eternity frozen in this dark nothing.

No. As the panic wore off and his surroundings came into sharper detail, Luke realized that he could still *feel* his arms and legs. He could even contract the muscles. He just couldn't move, not an inch. Some kind of warm, sticky slime was holding him in place. It was pulsing, squeezing him with a slow, steady rhythm. Like a heartbeat.

Suddenly, he knew exactly where he was. And the panic returned.

The last thing he'd seen was the beast's mouth closing over him. *I'm* inside *the creature,* Luke realized. *It ate me and now . . .*

And now what? Would he lie here encased in glop while the creature slowly digested him? For a moment, he wished he'd never woken up.

But he dismissed the thought. As long as he was alive, he could fight. He struggled to break free of the slime. If he could just reach his lightsaber, he could slice his way out. But his arm wouldn't budge. He was pinned tightly.

We're moving, Luke thought, his stomach lurching. *It feels like we're* falling.

He had no way to find out if that was true and no way to save himself. He was helpless.

It's not supposed to end this way, Luke thought angrily. *The Rebellion needs me. Leia needs me.*

Like I needed Ben, he thought. *And Aunt Beru. And Uncle Owen.*

All of them dead now, needed or not.

Luke struggled with renewed energy against the

gunk. Maybe he was doomed. But he wasn't about to give up. Until the very last moment, he would struggle. He would fight.

He would hope.

The chamber contracted. The walls crushed Luke in on himself. An iron grip seized his lungs, squeezing out his last breath. *This is it,* he thought.

And then he felt himself rolling through the slimy darkness and was flung into the light. The creature had vomited him up. Luke drew in a deep, heaving breath. He was lying on a flat bed of rock, coated with a sticky fluid. He was in a cave of some kind, with a deep pool at its center. The creature loomed over him, lips drawn back to reveal its jagged teeth. Luke whipped out his blaster and pulled the trigger. There was a soft pop, a fizzle of smoke — then nothing. He dropped the blaster and grabbed his lightsaber just as the creature shook its mighty head and slithered away. Before Luke could activate the weapon, the beast had disappeared into the water.

Luke clipped the lightsaber back to his belt and climbed to his feet. He wasn't alone. The remaining enemy pilot lay on his side, gasping and heaving. It sounded like he was coughing up his organs. Luke knelt by his side. "Are you all right?"

The man shook him off and pushed himself into a sitting position. "I've been swallowed by a giant . . . whatever-that-was and expelled into its blasted lair," he said in a rasping voice. He drew in a few more deep breaths, then stood up. "Does that seem all right to you?"

The cave was small and dark, with stalactites overhead that reminded Luke of the creature's jagged teeth. A foul stench clogged the air, but he couldn't be sure whether that was coming from the cave or from the slime that coated him from head to toe.

"The creature escaped through there," Luke said, pointing at the pool of water. "There must be some kind of opening to the outside." They didn't have much choice but to follow its example.

Luke jumped first, hoping the beast wouldn't be waiting for him. Holding his breath, he dived down through a wide underwater tunnel, trusting it would lead him back up to the surface. But instead, it released him into the open sea. Luke looked up, but he was too deep to even see the surface. Everywhere he looked, the world was only water.

A tightening in his chest made him realize he'd be out of air soon. He'd only recently learned how to swim. But even a champion swimmer wouldn't be able to hold his breath long enough to make it up to the surface. He had no choice but to turn back the way he'd come. Back to the cave.

Luke burst out of the water with no breath to spare. He drew in several lungfuls of the clammy cave air, grateful to breathe again. The pilot pulled himself back up onto the rocks next to Luke, not breathing nearly as hard. At least the water had washed away most of the slime.

"It must be an underwater sea cave," the pilot said. "An air pocket deep underwater. No way we'll make it back up there on our own. Not alive, at least."

"So that's it?" Luke said, frustrated. "We're trapped here forever? Why didn't that thing just eat us? Why dump us here to wait for us to starve to death?"

"I don't know why we're here, but I think we have more pressing concerns."

"What?" Luke followed the pilot's gaze, hoping he'd found another way out.

But the pilot wasn't looking at an escape route. He was looking at a large pile wedged into a niche in the cave. It was a heap of garbage. Seaweed, decaying sea grass, rotted fruit cores, ragged strips of plasteel, and lying on top —

Luke looked away, horrified. "Is that . . . ?"

"Grish B'reen," the pilot said. "Or at least . . . it was."

The Chistori was dead. His body, or what was left of it, had been torn to pieces. And it looked like they'd been partially . . . *digested*.

"I don't think that beast brought us here to die," the pilot said. "I think this is its nest and it's keeping us around until it's hungry again. Like the cavern spiders of Dathomir. I think it likes to *snack*. And that means when dinnertime comes around . . ."

"We better not be here anymore," Luke said, glancing back and forth between the water and the Chistori's remains. "One way or another."

alm down, you hairy oaf!" Han shouted at Chewbacca, who was howling with sorrow and rage. He shook his head. Was there anything more pathetic than a weeping Wookiee? "Luke's gone," he said, choking on the words. "There's nothing we can do about that. We have to focus on saving ourselves."

Chewbacca let out a few more snuffling hoots, but he followed Han deeper into the research station. According to the map, they weren't far from the docking bay. If they found a working ship, they'd be off the planet in no time. If not . . . well, Han decided not to think about that until he had to.

Just like he wouldn't think about Luke, swallowed up by that giant beast. Gone forever. All because Han had turned his back for a moment, had let Luke die.

Focus, Han reminded himself angrily. *Escape first, guilt later.*

They stuck to the plan, crept through the dark corridors, eyes and ears peeled for anything out of the ordinary. For slurping tentacles, for gnashing teeth, for drops of water spattering to the floor. Han gripped his blaster, almost hoping that the creature would find them. It had taken Luke — and for that, it deserved to die.

But the station was silent, the corridors empty. Their footsteps echoed. Their breath fogged in the chill air. It began to seem like they were wandering in circles, like they would be trapped in the hollow station forever. They rounded a corner, and there it was: the docking bay.

"Ships!" Han cried. Of course, from the look of things, they barely deserved the name. But he knew from experience that you couldn't judge a ship by its rusty frame. Plenty of fools had underestimated the *Millennium Falcon*.

The Kaminoans had left behind only their oldest, most battle-scarred ships, but at least a handful of them looked to be spaceworthy. Han spotted two Howlrunners with minimal scorching on the hull. Behind them, coated in grime, was an ARC-170 fighter, a distant ancestor of the Rebel X-wings. Those hadn't been flown since the Clone Wars, and rumor had it they'd been the ship of choice for the Republic's top pilots. Han had always wanted to take one for a spin. He didn't know what a ship like this would be doing way out on Kamino, but he wasn't about to let the opportunity go to waste.

Han jerked his head toward one of the Howlrunners. "Chewie, you check that one. I'll take the ARC."

It took only moments to figure out the rudimentary control system. The ship wouldn't have the power or the maneuverability of the X-wing, but the hyperdrive was powerful enough to make it back to Yavin 4, and that was all that mattered. He powered up the engines and navigational systems. Everything checked out. System diagnostics didn't indicate any problems. Chewbacca reported the same about the Howlrunner.

"You know what this means, don't you, buddy?" Han exclaimed. "We're going home."

Chewbacca barked a mournful reply.

"You're right," Han said quietly. "*Some* of us are going home."

Sorry, kid, he thought, a silent apology to Luke. *Wish you were coming with us.*

But Luke would remain on Kamino forever.

They couldn't take off without retrieving R2-D2, even though it meant risking another face-to-face with the dripping sea monster. They made it back to the central computer terminal safely. There was just one problem: R2-D2 had plans of his own. And they didn't include the docking bay.

"I said, *let's go,* you rustbucket!" Han shouted for a third time. But the little astromech droid just beeped and wheeled in exuberant circles. It was like his logic circuits had melted. He beeped again, louder this time, then rolled halfway down the hall before spinning around and returning to Han. His manipulator arm zigzagged through the air.

Chewbacca growled.

"I *know* he's trying to tell me something," Han snapped. "I just don't know *what*." And he wasn't in the mood for guessing games. Maybe the little guy was just upset about Luke being missing. "Come on, pal," he said in a gentler voice, trying not to lose his temper. "Whatever you have to tell us, it can wait."

R2-D2 beeped something that could have been a yes; then he began wheeling speedily down the hall.

"You see that?" Han said triumphantly, grinning at Chewbacca. "You've just got to know how to talk to — *hey!*"

The astromech droid had turned off the main corridor and was heading down a dark, narrow hallway, *away* from the docking bay.

"Where are you going?" Han shouted. "Come back here!"

If it had been up to him, he'd have ditched the blasted thing. Saving R2-D2 from his own foolishness wasn't worth it. But . . .

"Luke would never forgive us if we left the little guy behind," Han said wearily. Chewbacca was already down the hall in pursuit of the droid. Han shook his head and followed. "I'm only doing this for you, Luke," he muttered. He could just imagine the look on Luke's face if his precious astromech droid were abandoned on Kamino.

But thinking about that just led him to imagine *Leia's* face when she heard what had happened to Luke. When she heard what Han had *allowed* to happen to Luke.

"She'll never forgive me." Han stared at the ground, wishing the sea monster would appear again. Shooting at things always made him feel better.

R2-D2 came to a stop in front of a narrow transparisteel door. He plugged his manipulator arm into the control panel by the door and began fiddling with the circuits. A moment later, the door slid open.

"What are you doing?" A thin, warbling voice echoed through the hallway. "Shut that door! Shut it! Shut it! *Noooooooow!*" The voice turned into a howl. Without thinking, Han shoved Chewbacca and the droid through the door. It slid closed behind them with a solid clank.

They were in a cramped, narrow space, a little larger than a storage closet. Its shelves and tables were cluttered with test tubes, datapads, and other scientific detritus. And they weren't alone.

A gaunt, aged Kaminoan huddled in a corner of the room, fingers flying furiously across the keys of a large computer. He was tall and emaciated, with pale, luminescent white skin and bulging gray eyes that filled nearly half of his face. An inverted triangle, his head narrowed at the chin, held erect on a neck that was nearly as long and thin as his spindly arms. He was draped in a tattered lab coat that had faded to a dusty gray. "Who are you?" His voice was creaky and hesitant, like it hadn't been used for quite some time.

"Who are *you*?" Han shot back.

The Kaminoan stood up, brushing himself off. He stepped in front of a large computer console, blocking the screen from view. "I am Elo Panil." There was a haughty undertone to the words. "This is my research station — which would make you trespassers."

"Don't worry," Han said. "We're on our way out."

Chewbacca barked a suggestion.

Han sighed. On the one hand, this scientist had been working for the Empire. On the other hand, he couldn't leave an innocent man there to die. "You can come with us, if you'd like."

"Come with you?" The Kaminoan gaped at them, wild-eyed. "And leave my research behind? Are you mad?" He shook his head and turned his back to the intruders. Then he stepped aside, revealing the images playing across the wide screen. They were grainy black-and-white shots of the research station. "I've been watching you," the scientist said. He rubbed his spindly fingers nervously along the ridges at the base of his skull. "You're interfering with the experiment. I can't have impurities in my research, I simply can't. That would be very bad indeed."

Han and Chewbacca exchanged incredulous glances. "*Experiment?*" Han asked. "That's what you call that thing?"

"Certainly. And a successful one, at that." The Kaminoan faced them again, smiling proudly. "Who in the galaxy is more skilled in genetic manipulation? No one. Our clones have proven that, without doubt."

"Without doubt," Han muttered, grimacing. "Congratulations."

The Kaminoan didn't pick up on the sarcasm. "Thank you. So of course when the Empire came to us with their latest request, we were honored. They needed an organic superweapon to squelch resistance in a number of ground wars. So we set to work creating the ultimate beast."

"But things went wrong," Han said, prompting him.

"Wrong? *Wrong?*" The scientist's voice took on its first hint of real emotion. He was insulted. "To the contrary, they went *right*. The beast was everything we could have hoped for — and more. We never guessed how deadly such a creature could be. How efficient. And if my other, more timid colleagues preferred to run for their lives, instead of completing our work . . ."

"So that's where everyone went?" It was just as he'd thought. "They fled . . . the beast?"

"Some fled. Others . . ." The Kaminoan flicked a long, spindly hand, as if their fates were of no consequence to him. "Well, they learned firsthand the triumph of our creation."

"And you've been here ever since," Han said. "Watching."

The Kaminoan nodded. "I have food. I have my research. What else could I possibly need?"

How about a straitjacket? Han thought. But he kept his mouth shut.

Pleased to have an audience for his brilliance, the Kaminoan had begun muttering about all the marvelous capacities he'd built into the beast. "Armored skin. Durasteel piercing claws. Night vision. A venomous sting. The beast can kill a man in seconds, or transport living prisoners, when required. Now, *that* was a tricky one."

"What was that?" Han asked, suddenly paying attention again. "Prisoner transportation?"

"Of course, of course," the Kaminoan said eagerly. "A prickly problem indeed. The ultimate weapon is a flexible weapon, yes? The Empire wanted the capacity to capture and transport prisoners alive, when necessary. Difficult, yes? Not so difficult, as it turns out. Maybe creatures deliver their food to the nest intact, feasting on it at leisure. Or offering it as a communal food source. Brillizards, tropotaurs, the cavern spiders of Dathomir —"

"Enough!" Han exclaimed. "You mean when the beast eats someone, they don't die?"

"Not always, no," the Kaminoan said. "Some prey is transported, alive, in the creature's stomach, to the feeding ground."

"The beast swallowed my friend," Han said, hardly daring to hope. "Do you think . . . he could still be alive?"

There was a long pause.

"Possible," the Kaminoan said finally.

Chewbacca let out a joyous howl.

"Of course, the delivery mechanism was never *quite* perfected. We had certain problems with suffocation. And acidic decomposition."

Chewbacca released another howl, this one less enthused.

"Look on the bright side," the Kaminoan said reassuringly. "At least if your friend died in transit, he won't be alive when the beast begins to feed."

Han wanted to throttle the scientist. "That's our *friend* you're talking about," he said. "What's wrong with you?"

"The only thing wrong with me is that you're interrupting my research," the Kaminoan said.

R2-D2 beeped.

"You're right, we're wasting time," Han said. "Look, we're going to go rescue our friend, and then we're leaving this planet. We can take you along, if you want."

"All I want is to be left alone," the scientist said, turning his back on them again.

"Suit yourself." Han slammed a fist into the control panel, and the door slid open.

"I'd advise you to forget your friend," the Kaminoan said, hunching over his computer. "He's lost to you."

"Which means you don't know where the sea monster would've taken him," Han said.

"Of course not," the Kaminoan straightened. "My creation is far too brilliant to let anyone know where its lair is located."

"Well, we're not going anywhere without Luke," Han said. "We arrived together; we'll leave together."

The Kaminoan shook with a harsh, ragged chuckle. "You'll die together."

Han shot him one last sour glance before the door slipped shut. "Better than dying alone."

iv dumped his blaster in disgust. Maybe the seawater had flooded it; maybe something corrosive in the creature's innards had damaged it. Either way, it no longer worked. They were weaponless. And trapped. But not helpless.

Div never allowed himself to be helpless.

"That *thing* could be back soon," he told Luke, who was gazing into the water as if it would yield the secret of their salvation. "There must be something around here we can turn into a weapon." He started sifting through the damp, moss-covered rocks, careful to keep his back to the pile of debris and Chistori remains. He hadn't let himself wonder about what had happened to Clea's body. Maybe the beast only saved its food after it had been fully sated by an earlier meal. Maybe Clea's death had saved their lives.

Or maybe she was there after all, resting in pieces, beneath Grish.

Div had never thought of himself as a squeamish person. And something might be buried in the detritus that could serve as a weapon. Grish's blaster might even have made it through intact. But Div just couldn't bring himself to look. Not yet. "Well?" he snapped at Luke. "You going to stand there and daydream, or you going to help me find a weapon?"

Luke jerked his eyes away from the water. "When that thing comes back, I'll be ready." He pulled a slim gray rod from beneath his coat. A beam of blue light blazed from the base.

Div's eyes widened. He felt all his breath sucked out of him, like he was back in the creature's belly again. And in an instant, he was on top of Luke, his hand around the Rebel's throat. The lightsaber dropped to the ground and rolled a few feet away.

"Get off me!" Luke shouted, but Div only tightened his hold. He dragged Luke off the ground and pinned him to the cave wall, banging his head against the rocks. "Where'd you get it?" he growled. "The lightsaber?"

"It's mine," Luke gasped, trying to suck in more air. Div's fingers tightened around his windpipe.

"The truth," Div whispered harshly. "Jedi leave their lightsabers behind only in death. So are you a thief or a murderer? Or *both*?"

Luke stopped his feeble attempts to escape. Instead, he squeezed his eyes shut and stretched a hand toward

93

the lightsaber. Div watched him for a moment in disbelief. Was the Rebel pilot actually trying to *summon* the lightsaber? Was he trying to access . . . the Force?

"One more time," Div said, watching Luke carefully. He would recognize a lie when he saw it. "Where did you find the Jedi weapon?"

"My father," Luke choked out. "It belonged to my father."

Div searched Luke's face. The Rebel's expression was as sincere as his voice. But Div didn't need the confirmation. He knew it was the truth. Maybe he'd known since the first time he'd seen Luke, that moment in the lab when Luke had disappeared inside himself. The truth was in the way Luke moved, the way he held himself. And when Div released him, the truth was in the way Luke snatched the lightsaber from the ground and held it to himself. After checking it for damage, he activated the blade and faced Div.

His grip was clumsy, his stance unbalanced, but there was no mistaking it: This was Luke's rightful weapon.

Which could mean only one thing.

"This lightsaber belonged to my father, and now it belongs to me," Luke said, his tone a warning.

Weapon or not, Div could have disarmed him easily. But he had no desire to do so. Not anymore. "Your father was a Jedi," Div said quietly. It wasn't a question.

Luke nodded. "And so am I."

The young man actually sounded *proud.*

"All you are is a blasted fool," Div spat, "if you think being a Jedi is anything other than a death sentence."

Luke advanced with the lightsaber. Div held up his hands. "No need," he said calmly. "You have nothing to fear from me. But out there . . ." He gestured to the water, to the wider galaxy, where a man would have to be insane to label himself a Jedi. "You have no idea what kind of misery you're going to attract."

"You know about the Jedi?" Luke asked searchingly with a hopeful note in his voice.

"No."

"But you said—"

"I know only what everyone else knows," Div said tersely. "The Jedi are dead and gone. All of them."

"Not all of them," Luke said.

"Not yet."

"But—" Before Luke could persist with his annoying questions, the water rippled and churned. The creature surfaced, dragging itself onto the rocks with giant tentacles. Luke raised the lightsaber and rushed at the beast.

"Luke, no!" Div shouted.

But Luke ignored him and slashed at the creature with rough, clumsy strokes. The beast moaned in pain once, twice, proof that Luke had made glancing contact with his thick hide. But then a thick tentacle slashed the air, slamming hard into Luke's stomach. The aspiring Jedi flew backward across the cave, his lightsaber sailing in the opposite direction. Div darted forward, snatching the weapon in midair.

As if sensing the danger, the creature turned toward him. Div was ready. It should have felt strange to hold a lightsaber again. And in a way, it was. The hilt seemed too small in his hand, too light. He overcompensated at first, swinging hard against the creature and nearly stumbling when the blade met little resistance. But the confusion, the clumsiness, it lasted no more than a second or two. Then . . . it was like coming home. The blade danced wildly, lighting up the dim cave. He ducked beneath a swinging tentacle, leapt over another one. The blade sliced through the tentacles like they were made of air. The creature shrieked in rage and pain, its keens echoing through the cave as Div lashed out with the blade once, twice — again and again.

He didn't stop until the cries faded to silence and the creature was dead on the ground, sliced into pieces. When he looked up, Luke was staring at him in astonishment.

"Where did you learn how to do that?" Luke asked in a hushed voice.

Div shrugged. "What's to learn? It's just a blade, like any other."

"But I thought only a Jedi could —"

"I don't care what you think," Div said stiffly. "I've been around. I've seen this kind of weapon before. That's all, nothing more." He looked down at the lightsaber. It was so much more graceful than a blaster, so much more deadly. And for just a moment, he was tempted to claim it as his own.

But that would mean claiming far more than the weapon, and the time for that had passed long ago.

"Here," he said, and tossed the lightsaber to Luke. "This is yours. Take better care of it this time."

"Were you trained by Jedi?" Luke asked eagerly. "Who were they? What were they like? Are any of them still . . . ?"

Alive, Div thought. *That's what he wants to ask, but he can't bring himself to say the word. Because he knows the answer.* "The past is past," he said. "I don't talk about it."

"But why do you—" Luke caught the steely expression on Div's face and cut himself off. He cleared his throat. "You could at least tell me your name," he said after a moment. "Or is that part of the secret past, too?"

"Div," he said, because that was the name he'd gone by for nearly two decades. But then he hesitated. If Luke knew about the Jedi, what else did he know about? "Lune Divinian," he said carefully, watching Luke's face for a flicker of recognition. *Something.* But there was nothing.

And Div found he was disappointed.

He shook it off. "So, we're not going to be eaten anytime soon," he said, approaching the dead beast. "All that means is a long, boring death, unless we can figure a way out of here. Of course, there could be more than one."

"What if we went *out* the same way we came *in*," Luke mused.

"We're trying to *avoid* being breakfast," Div reminded him. "And even if the thing weren't dead, I don't speak monster well enough to request that it not digest us this time around. Do you?"

Luke ignored the taunt. "We know its stomach is airtight," he said, "and can hold enough air for us to breathe until we reach the surface. So if we could find a way to use it, turn it into some kind of waterproof casing—"

"Like a submarine," Div said, suddenly hopeful. The so-called Jedi was smarter than he looked.

"You think it could work?"

Div couldn't help sneaking a look at Grish's dead body and at the moss-covered bones littering the floor of the cave. "I think it has to."

CHAPTER
ELEVEN

"Y ou sure this gadget's going to work?" Han asked as R2-D2 put the finishing touches on the modified tracking device.

The droid beeped irritably and continued his work.

"Well, hurry it along," Han said impatiently.

Chewbacca issued a warning growl.

"How do *you* know he's doing the best he can?" Han asked. "That bucket of bolts acts like we have all the time in the world."

R2-D2 beeped again, and Chewbacca barked at Han.

"No, I *won't* admit that we wouldn't have found the scientist if it weren't for him. I had a feeling there was someone else on the station. Besides, even a laser-brain could have guessed that Luke might still be alive somewhere."

Chewbacca didn't even dignify that with an answer. Han ignored the Wookiee and concentrated on the astromech droid. He knew that yelling at R2-D2 wasn't going to speed things up, but he couldn't help himself. He was impatient. The longer they hung around, the greater chance that the beast would return.

Of course, that was what they were hoping for — but not yet. Not until they were ready.

R2-D2 whistled triumphantly and held the modified tracker out to Han. He examined the device. Even he had to admit that it was nice work. Especially considering that all the droid had to work with were the homing beacons from the left-over Kaminoan craft. "You sure this will work?"

The droid beeped and wheeled across the room, indicating that it was time for the next phase of their plan. Han took a deep breath and followed. This was it: If the plan worked, the beast would eat the tracker. If not, it would eat Han.

Han grinned. *Either way, kid, looks like I'll be seeing you soon.*

Han shifted his weight, trying not to seem nervous. What was there to be nervous about? So he was sitting in the middle of the abandoned laboratory, carefully positioned near the pool of still, dark water, waiting for a disgusting sea creature to attack. So what?

"Any day now, you slimesucker," Han muttered, wondering what was taking so long. *Maybe it only feeds once a day,* he thought. *Or once a month.*

But he pushed those doubts out of his mind. This had to work. Luke was counting on him.

The water rippled.

Han tensed, blaster in one hand, homing beacon in the other.

A massive scaled snout emerged, jaws wide, jagged teeth gleaming in the dim light. Han took an involuntary step back, then steadied himself. This plan depended on split-second timing. He couldn't run away, not until the time was right.

The creature slithered out of the water, its tentacles slapping hard against the durasteel floor. It reared up, scenting prey. Han froze as the beast loomed over him. He'd never been this close before. But now he could see the black pupils pooling in wide eyes, the drops of water trickling down its thick, pitted hide, the sharp stingers embedded along its tentacles, the deep, dark gully of its throat as it opened its jaws improbably wide and swooped down . . .

Chewbacca's panicked howl snapped Han out of his horrified trance.

"Now!" Han shouted.

Chewbacca fired a burst of laserfire straight at the creature's mouth. As it let loose an agonized howl, Han drew back his arm and pitched the tracking device straight into the creature's gaping maw. Before it could recover, he scampered out of the way, racing for the other side of the room. Chewbacca kept firing, careful to aim for the beast's tentacles and armored torso. The last thing they wanted now was to kill the creature before it led them back to Luke.

As the beast screeched and writhed in the hail of laserfire, searching in vain for its attacker, Han crept out of the laboratory and locked the door shut behind him. He joined Chewbacca, who was aiming his blaster through a narrow hole they'd drilled in the wall.

"Enough," Han said quietly.

The Wookiee stopped firing, and Han peered through the hole, eager to see what the creature would do next. It slithered around the laboratory, searching for something—someone—to eat. Maybe it smelled Han, or maybe it spotted his eye flickering behind the hole in the wall, because it edged closer and closer to his hiding spot, flattening its head against the hole. Han flinched and drew back. The beast slammed a tentacle against the wall, and another. Han held his breath, his hands tight around the blaster. He didn't want to kill the beast.

But he wasn't about to die in its place.

The creature was strong, but the durasteel was stronger. The wall held.

The laboratory had other exits. If the creature was determined to find its prey, it could slither off in another direction and search the station. Han prepared himself for a long spukamas and mouse game. But instead, the beast snuffled and grunted, then slipped back into the water. It submerged with a splash, and was gone.

Chewbacca growled a question.

"How should I know, pal?" Han said. "Long day of stalking people — maybe it's just tired."

Maybe it's just full. But that fell into the category of things he wouldn't allow himself to think about. Nothing could be done if Luke was dead. But as long as there was even a chance that the kid was still alive, Han had to push forward.

Once they were sure the creature wasn't coming back, Chewbacca and Han joined R2-D2 before a large monitor. The screen lit with a map of the city. *If* the droid had programmed the tracker correctly, *if* it hadn't malfunctioned in the creature's gullet, *if* the beast returned to his feeding ground, *if* Luke was still alive . . .

There were a lot of ifs. But Han was a gambler; ifs were what made life fun.

"Come on, you blasted beast," he muttered. "Take us home."

They waited for the tracker's blinking light to appear on the screen.

They waited a long, painful moment. And another.

"I see it!" Han shouted as a small green light appeared and inched slowly across the map. "The overgrown slug's showing us exactly where to go!"

He gave R2-D2 a dome-rattling slap on the back.

Chewbacca released a worried growl, tracing a furry paw across the screen. Han winced. "You're right; it's headed for the sea." He'd seen some Roamer-6 breath masks in the supply room when they were rummaging for spare parts for the tracking device. It was the same model they carried on the *Falcon,* because unlike most rebreathers, it could fit a Wookiee. Breathing underwater would be the easy part. Sure, they could swim down in search of the creature's lair — but it was hard to fight underwater, and their blasters would be useless. So how were they supposed to rescue Luke without becoming meals themselves?

If only there was some way to be on equal footing with the creature. Some way to turn the water to their advantage . . .

"That's it!" Han shouted suddenly as a rough plan began to coalesce. Chewbacca barked excitedly. Han shook his head. "No time to explain. I'll tell you on the way." He turned to the astromech droid. "Stay here and ready the ships. Chewie and I will be back soon — and so will Luke. We're finally blasting off this rock. *All* of us."

CHAPTER TWELVE

Luke guided the lightsaber along the seam of flesh, cauterizing the edge. "I think that does it," he said, surveying their work. He and Div had sliced the beast open and crafted a large, lumpy, misshapen bubble out of its massive stomach cavern. The result was a semitranslucent container with just enough space for two humans. If they were lucky, it would keep the air in and the water out. Luke had done most of the work, as he wasn't about to let Div take the lightsaber again. But Div hadn't asked. He'd seemed content to stand by as Luke sliced and diced the creature, helping Luke stretch and press the flesh into a shape they could use.

Luke still didn't trust the man. But he was grateful for the help.

"You ready?" he asked.

"Always," Div said.

They climbed into the bubble and, using the heat of the lightsaber to melt the edges together, sealed themselves inside. Now there was no time to spare. The bubble held a finite amount of air. Once it was gone, they were dead.

They had managed to shape the slimy flesh around their legs, giving them the flexibility to propel themselves forward. It might even allow them to steer. But they had no idea whether they'd have enough buoyancy to keep the bubble from sinking once it was out in the open sea. This was their last option. That didn't make it a good one.

Nodding at Div, Luke began to scrabble his feet against the cave rock, pushing them forward into the pool of water. They tipped over the edge with a splash. Luke braced himself, waiting for water to blow through the seams of the bubble, flooding them before they could even begin. But the membrane held. A mild current carried them slowly through the tunnel of water, drawing them into the sea. Luke breathed shallowly, trying not to worry about how much air they had left. He had survived the journey down from the surface. They had no reason to believe there wouldn't be enough air to make it in the opposite direction.

The bubble slowly rose toward the surface. Schools of orange-and-gray-striped fish skittered out of the way. They floated past rocky outcroppings of rainbow-colored corals, spindly branches alive with tiny creatures. Long tendrils of seaweed swayed with the current; bright eyes gleamed from behind the undulating green curtain.

Gradually, the water took on a dim glow. They were nearing the surface.

This is actually going to work, Luke thought.

That was before a shadow passed over them like a storm cloud. A well of dread pooling in the pit of his stomach, Luke looked up. He gasped.

It was another of the beasts. It glided through the water, its thick tentacles trailing behind it. Luke gripped his lightsaber.

"Are you insane?" Div hissed. "You slice this thing open, we drown."

"That thing comes for us, we're dead anyway," Luke shot back, though he knew that Div was right. He holstered the weapon. "What should we do?"

But Div, who'd been acting like he had all the answers, was silent.

"Maybe it won't see us," Luke said.

"Maybe we should paddle back to the cave," Div suggested.

"Back?" Luke exclaimed. "But we're so close!"

"We can't fight. We can't hide. What do you want to do?" Div sighed. "Sometimes you have to play it safe."

Sometimes these days, it felt like playing it safe was all Luke ever did. But maybe Div was right. What other option did they have?

"Now," Div urged him, "before that *thing* realizes we're here. We can always try again."

They began paddling back toward the mouth of the cave. But the bubble was too buoyant, and the current too strong. No matter what they did, they kept floating up — toward the surface, toward the creature. "This isn't working," Luke said nervously, looking up at the underbelly of the beast. "And if it senses that we're here —"

"I think we may have bigger problems," Div said quietly.

Luke looked away from the creature. His mouth dropped open.

The thick membrane of the bubble gave everything a fogged, shadowy look, turning the world into a collage of blurs melting into one another. But the shapes approaching them were clear enough. Another of the creatures, and another. On the ground, they had been fast but awkward. Underwater, they moved with a deadly grace, tentacles cutting through the sea as they glided toward their prey. Luke glanced behind them; more of the creatures were swarming. There had to be at least ten of them, and in the distance, he spotted more on the way.

They were surrounded.

hat'd I tell you?" Han said. "The answer to our prayers!"

Chewbacca looked dubiously at the nest of aiwhas, then back at Han. He barked a question.

"Easy," Han said confidently. "We just . . . ride them."

Chewbacca barked again.

"Well, I don't know *how* we're going to do it," Han said irritably. "But standing around *whining* about it isn't going to help." And it wasn't going to get Luke back. The aiwhas were their best shot, maybe their only shot. Han knew that the creatures had been tamed by the Kaminoans. Maybe since the city had been abandoned, they'd reverted to their wild origins, but any animal that had once allowed itself to be ridden would allow it again — assuming Han and Chewbacca could find a way to climb up on their backs.

Han looked up at the aiwha nest — way up.

The huge birdlike lizards swooped in wide circles around the spired building. Their wingspread was more than twice Han's height. And the muscles rippling in their massive tails looked powerful enough to knock the top off a building.

"Just like riding a bantha," Han said. "Not a problem."

Chewbacca didn't look convinced.

"We just need to find a way up there," Han mused.

Chewbacca growled a sharp retort.

"What do you mean you don't think that's our biggest problem?" Han asked. "What else do you — *whoaaaaaa!*" An aiwha, flying low, knocked him off his feet. "Not again," Han muttered, rubbing the new lump on his forehead. He looked up, watching the aiwha's tough underbelly as it circled through the air.

Maybe another little sky ride was exactly what he needed. It would sure beat climbing up to the nest. Han shouted and waved, trying to lure the aiwha closer. It wheeled low, crying out, and soon others joined it, all circling toward Han.

Now that they were closer, Han could see that only a couple of the creatures still had their harnesses. Han waited for his opening. Then with one last glance back at Chewbacca, Han reached up and clamped a hand around an aiwha's harness. It squawked in consternation, but Han held tightly as the ground dropped out beneath him. Now he was dangling in midair on the strength of the grip in his left hand.

The aiwha's hide was too leathery to offer any kind of handhold, but if he could wedge his hand into the niche between the wing and the torso, it was just possible he could pull himself onto the creature's back. He strained to pull himself up the creature's body, but there was no way. The torso was too wide, and he had no leverage. He needed some momentum, to give him an extra push.

Han began swinging his legs through the air, sweeping them rhythmically back and forth until his body swayed like a pendulum beneath the aiwha. He still didn't have the arm span to reach the wing — not as long as he was holding on to the harness. But there was something else he could try.

He swung back and forth as hard as he could. This had to be timed exactly right. If he missed, he would drop to the ground, which was now at least thirty meters below. But he had to at least *try*. "You better thank me for this one, kid," Han muttered, and — giving himself one last hard swing — let go.

For a terrifying, exhilarating moment, he was flying free. He stretched out his arms, straining toward the aiwha's wing. His fingertips caught hold of the edge, then slipped. He was going to fall.

Han scrabbled for purchase, clinging to the aiwha. Thrown off balance, the flying lizard tipped to the right, then flapped hard, trying to disengage its unwelcome visitor. Han clenched the wing as tightly as he could. Then, his biceps bulging with the strain, he pulled himself up so that his chest was level with the wing.

He curled his legs up to his chest and walked his feet up the side of the aiwha until he was nearly standing on the wing. Then it was a simple matter of flattening himself against the aiwha and carefully shinnying his way up the torso until he found himself squarely on the creature's back. It bucked angrily, its smooth flight transformed into a jerky, teeth-clattering mess of bumps and jolts. Han tried looping his legs through the creature's harness, but it had been built for a Kaminoan. So he wrapped his arms around its thick neck, squeezing tightly as the creature plunged into a perilous dive.

Han laced his fingers together and pulled gently against the aiwha's neck. It was a strategy he'd learned from breaking in wild rontos back on Corellia. And just like a ronto, the aiwha slowly relaxed into his command. "Thatta girl," Han said softly, patting the aiwha's long neck as it leveled out of its dive. He experimented with his control over the creature, tugging it gently to starboard, encouraging it to ascend steeply, then taking it into a shallow, controlled dive. He discovered that a quick, light kick to its haunches made the creature speed up, while pulling back on its shoulders slowed it down again. Han shook his head, grinning. "No such thing as a ship I can't fly."

Once he was sure of his control over the aiwha, he swung it toward the ground, heading straight for Chewbacca. They buzzed the Wookiee, skimming the air just over his head. Han waved cockily at his surprised friend. "What'd I tell you?" he shouted and brought the aiwha in for a landing a few meters away from the Wookiee. "Well, what are you waiting for?" he asked, slapping the aiwha's backside. "Hop on!"

Once they'd managed one aiwha, it was far simpler to capture a second one. Han and Chewbacca just rode the tamed lizard up to the nest. Chewbacca was easily able to hop off and land on the back of a second one. That aiwha fell into line just as quickly as the first.

They flew swiftly toward the edge of the city, following the flashing signal of the homing beacon on the handheld portable monitor in Han's hand. As they approached the water, Han slipped on his breath mask. Chewbacca did the same. The masks made it difficult to talk — and once they were underwater, difficult would become impossible. But Han and Chewbacca understood each other. When they'd reached the beast's underwater lair, there wouldn't be many options to discuss. Their blasters would be useless. They'd managed to scrounge a couple of concussion grenades from the research station supplies, but there was no telling if they were still functional. This was the kind of mission with a limited number of possible outcomes.

They would run, or they would fight.

They would fail, or they would succeed.

When they found Luke, he would be alive. Or he wouldn't.

The aiwhas plunged beneath the water. Han stiffened against the icy blast. He hadn't expected the cold. His muscles cramped up, but he held tightly to the aiwha, forcing it deeper and deeper into the sea.

The signal was closer, but the beast was on the move. Han slowed the aiwha as they drew near. The distant surface cast little light, but swarms of Kaminoan electro-eels gave the underwater world a dim glow. Han spotted the mouth of a cave in the distance and wondered if Luke was inside. But the signal had moved a half kilometer to the east, and Han decided to pursue that first. Chewbacca followed.

Suddenly, they both stopped cold. The aiwhas flung their wings out to halt their glide through the water, bucking and wriggling in fear. They had found the beast — and about twenty of the beast's closest friends.

And floating in the center of the ring of monsters: a large translucent bubble. Han narrowed his eyes, unable to believe what he was seeing. Two shadowy human figures inside the bubble. One lit by the telltale blue glow of a Jedi lightsaber.

Luke was alive — and he was in trouble.

Han didn't hesitate. He forced the balking aiwha forward, faster and faster. The beasts were advancing on Luke. Han had only one weapon at his disposal, and now was the time to use it. He fired a concussion grenade directly at the beast farthest from Luke. It detonated on impact. The creature — and the two beasts on either side of it — exploded in a storm of frothing water and thick, viscous red fluid. Han had been hoping the explosion would frighten the creatures away. But the scent of blood drove them into a fury. They set upon the drifting pieces of flesh in a squall of wriggling tentacles and gnashing teeth.

Luke used the lightsaber to slit open the skin of the bubble. He swam furiously toward Han, who did his best to calm the panicky aiwha before it decided Luke would make good comfort food. The enemy pilot swam after Luke, but Han waved his hands. He'd brought along only one extra breath mask and air tank. Luke shook his head, pointing at the pilot, then at Chewbacca's aiwha, making his meaning clear. He wasn't going to the surface unless the other pilot came along.

He took the mask Han handed him and held it over his mouth for a moment, then passed it to the other pilot, who took a breath and passed it back to Luke. Han got the idea. And there was no time to argue. They were running out of air. Soon the beasts would be done feasting on carrion and start looking for fresh blood. Han shrugged and directed the enemy pilot to Chewbacca's aiwha. Luke forced him to take the mask. Han drew in a deep breath and handed his own mask to Luke. If the aiwha swam fast enough, they could make it back to the surface, switching off every few seconds.

He urged the aiwha to ascend, feeling like his lungs would burst. Soon Luke handed the breather back. They swapped it back and forth, streaking toward the surface. Han glanced back once, to see the horde of beasts swimming after them. He decided not to look again. They sped through the water, schools of tiny fish darting away from the aiwha's massive wings.

Breaking through the surface was like waking from a nightmare. Even the storm-darkened Kamino skies were a welcome change from the unrelieved darkness of the sea. Han sucked in a deep, cleansing breath of fresh air and directed the aiwha back toward the research station. They were finally on their way home.

"You okay, kid?" Han asked as they glided through the city.

"I don't understand," Luke said, gripping the aiwha tightly. "How did you find us?"

"What makes you think I was looking for you?" Han joked. "Maybe Chewie and I just felt like doing some fishing."

"You saved my life," Luke said, craning forward in an attempt to meet Han's eye.

"I suggest you hang on," Han grinned as they dived toward the surface of the planet. The research station was only a hundred meters away. "Pretty soon we'll be —"

"Duck!" Luke shouted, flattening Han against the aiwha. A blast of laserfire screamed past them. The aiwha shrieked as another blast scorched its tail. A row of Imperial assault tanks had assembled in front of the research station. Each was equipped with a rotating laser cannon and dual missile launchers — all of which were aimed at Han and Luke.

A concussion grenade dropped out of the sky, blowing one of the tanks to bits. A hailstorm of flak erupted from the wreckage. Han glanced up at Chewie, who'd tossed the grenade. "Thanks, pal!" he shouted. Chewbacca roared back, then pulled out his blaster and began firing at the tanks.

Han and Luke did the same, but it was useless; the tanks' deflector shields could easily bear the blasterfire. And pretty soon, one of the Imperial missiles would score a direct hit.

"Can't this thing fly any higher?" Luke shouted. "We have to get away!"

"I'm working on it!" Han said irritably, trying to come up with a better option. They could fly away on the aiwhas, all right, but then what? They ships they needed were inside the research station — which meant that if they ever wanted to go home, they had to find a way past those tanks.

And they had to do it before the tanks blew them out of the sky.

Luke hunched down, firing his blaster at the tanks as Han steered the aiwha. They wheeled in circles, trying to avoid the enemy fire. Rain pelted their faces. Gusts of wind buffeted them from side to side. A missile screamed past, too close for comfort. The aiwha bucked. Luke lost his grip on the slippery hide. He lurched forward, sliding down the creature's back.

Han seized his wrist, hauling him upright. "Hold on tight, kid," he shouted, trying to make himself heard over the rushing wind. "This is gonna be bumpy!"

They zigzagged through the streams of laserfire, riding the updraft higher and higher. The atmosphere thinned. Bolts of lightning sizzled, uncomfortably close. But gradually the noise of battle faded, and the laserfire tapered off. As the ground disappeared beneath them, Luke realized they were hidden in the dense cloud cover.

Chewbacca followed their lead, guiding his aiwha up to Han's level. Soon they were flying side by side.

"That blasted scientist must have tipped them off," Han muttered. "I knew he was trouble."

Chewbacca's aiwha swooped in close enough that they could hear Div shouting. "What now?" he called.

"Ships are waiting for us in that station," Han shouted back. "We have to go back."

"We'll never make it past the tanks!" Luke pointed out. "They have too much firepower."

Han craned his neck around to grin at Luke. "You're exactly right. That's it."

"What's it?" Luke asked, confused.

"We'll give them something else to fire at," Han said. He waved at Chewbacca. "Come on!"

Luke held on more tightly as the aiwha dived through the clouds. The ground screamed toward them. The Imperial tanks charged up their weapons and began firing again. Han hooted in triumph. "That's right, boys!" he shouted, shaking a fist at the tanks. "Come and get us!"

The aiwha veered sharply to the right, heading away from the research station. "Han, what are you doing?" Luke shouted. "We're going the wrong way!"

Han ignored him and pushed the aiwha faster. They rode low over the city, banking and weaving to avoid the laserfire. Luke quickly realized they were backtracking, heading to the point where they'd come ashore. They soon approached the sea. The water rippled and churned, spitting up froth along the shore. Han took the aiwha lower and lower, until they were nearly skimming the surface. "What are you doing?" Luke asked again, peering nervously into the dark water.

"See those maneuvering fins on the tanks?" Han asked as they glided back and forth across the water, about ten meters over on the sea. "Those tanks are amphibious. They want us, they're going to have to follow us. And there's a nasty surprise waiting if they do."

He was right — at least about the first part. The tanks didn't even pause as they reached the landing platform. Mechanical fins extended like wings, and repulsorlifts retracted as the tanks shifted to a jet propulsion system. The armored vehicles rolled off the ramp at the platform's end and into the water, their jets keeping them afloat. A constant stream of laserfire burst from the water. The aiwha screamed as a blast scalded its hind legs. The creature lurched in the air, its wings flapping unevenly. Luke tried not to think about what would happen if it took another hit. They were close enough to the water that the fall wouldn't kill them. But he wasn't worried about the fall. He was worried about what lay beneath.

Except they weren't beneath, not anymore. The water around the tanks began to churn. Black tentacles emerged from the waves, slapping against the durasteel hulls. Within seconds, the sea came alive with wriggling bodies, tentacles and jaws and iridescent armored flanks glittering in the laser light. The tanks stopped firing at the aiwhas. Luke stared down in horror as they lowered their laser cannons toward the water, trying to put the sea monsters down. But it was no use. One missile slammed into another tank, tearing a hole through its hull. The tank filled with water and began to sink. Faint screams drifted up from the sea.

Han had lost his smile. He and Luke watched somberly as the creatures swarmed in a frenzy. There couldn't have been more than twenty of them, but it seemed like hundreds. The tanks tried to escape, but they were surrounded. Tentacles wrapped around missile launchers, maneuvering fins, shield generators—dragging the tanks down. And slowly but surely, they sank beneath the surface. One after another, they disappeared into the choppy sea, until nothing was left of them but a few rising bubbles and a single tentacle slithering into the deep.

Then the sea was empty. The tanks were gone.

And beneath the surface, the beasts fed.

"We had no choice," Luke said quietly.

"We had no choice," Han repeated, his voice flat. He turned the aiwha toward the research station without another word. Neither of them looked back.

It took only a few minutes to return to the center of the city. Luke tipped his head toward the sky, letting frigid rain stream down his face. Storm clouds swirled overhead. Thunder boomed so loudly it felt like the storm was right on top of them. The rumbling grew louder, and a blinding flash of light pierced the clouds. *That wasn't lightning,* Luke thought.

"Han, incoming at three o'clock!" he shouted as a laser bolt went screaming past. Just beneath them, a building exploded, slamming them with a powerful shock wave.

Chewbacca and Div barely avoided the leaping flames.

"Got to get this bird on the ground," Han cried as a squadron of TIE fighters burst through the clouds. He drove the aiwha forward until the research station came into sight; then he launched them into a precariously steep dive. All around them, explosions rattled the city. The TIE fighters fanned out, swooping shockingly close to the ground. Luke had faced the ships plenty of times before, but never without the protection of his own X-wing. Now, hurtling through the air completely exposed, he shuddered at the swarm of fighters. They weren't just ships; they were death machines.

"Quit dreaming, kid, and prepare to jump," Han shouted, bringing the aiwha in for a landing. "We have to get in and out of that station before the Empire blows it away."

The ships are in the far north wing!" Han shouted, leaping off the aiwha the moment its clawed paws touched the ground. He ran toward the building. Luke and the Wookiee followed close behind him, with Div bringing up the rear. "Follow me!"

"Hurry," Div yelled, "before —" A crack of thunder drowned him out. Div glanced up, expecting to see another storm swirling overhead. But the clouds had been replaced by a swarm of TIE fighters. "Incoming!" Div shouted, diving for cover as laserfire rained down on them. He shoved Luke out of the way just as the wall of a building exploded outward, showering the streets with a storm of flak.

The ground shook and shuddered as they raced toward the research station. Streaks of laserfire lit the sky. The air grew thick with smoke and ash. Div choked on the acrid stench of fire. He knew what would happen next. The Imperials would raze the city. Their attack would flatten the buildings and turn the remaining heaps of durasteel into an inferno. And then, when the ground was flat and lifeless, when there was nothing left — no motion, no sound, no hope — they would depart to wreak their destruction on another corner of the galaxy. They would leave behind nothing but corpses.

Broken bodies, like the bodies of his parents, their unseeing eyes clouded with blood.

Twisted shards of durasteel, like the smoldering remnants of the safe house, the last place he'd seen Trevor, before the Empire arrived.

And once again, they would leave him alive, alone. Surrounded by death. *Because that's my job, isn't it?* he thought wryly, refusing to allow the flood of self-pity. *I live, while all those around me die.*

The galaxy needs you, they had said, sacrificing themselves so that he could survive.

You are our hope.

But that hope had been crushed. Flattened, just like everything else.

No, he thought, furious with himself. This wasn't the time to lose oneself in memories. He was no one's salvation. And that boy, that *Lune,* no longer existed. He was Div now, nothing more. Lune was as dead as his parents, as dead as his adopted brother, as dead as all that *special, extraordinary potential* that so many had wasted their lives to protect.

Dead as I'm going to be if I don't snap out of it, Div thought irritably. They had reached the research station, and he threw himself inside, along with Luke, Han, and Chewbacca, slamming the door behind them. They pounded down the corridors toward the north docking bay. The walls rattled as laserfire strafed the roof. The building was taking a lot of hits, too many. "Won't be easy to take off in this," Div muttered.

"Easy's boring," Han shot back.

A chunk of the ceiling collapsed. Div and Han dived out of the way just as a heavy rock of duracrete crashed between them. "I'll take boring," Div muttered.

But that wasn't an option.

In minutes, they made it to the docking bay, where the astromech droid waited beside three dilapidated ships.

"Good job, Artoo!" Luke exclaimed, hurrying toward the ship on the far right, a rusted Imperial Howlrunner with scorch marks along its fixed wings.

"The more ships, the more firepower," Han said, "so . . ."

"Agreed," Div said brusquely. Han was right; they needed as many ships on their side as possible. But no matter what, Div wouldn't have trusted anyone's piloting skills but his own. He chose the other Howlrunner, on the left, while Han and the Wookiee piled into the ARC-170 starfighter.

Han began to power up his ship. Luke's engines were hot and ready to go. But Div took an extra moment to inspect the exterior of his Howlrunner, making sure there was no obvious damage or hull breach; he even found a replacement for his defunct weapon in an inside compartment—a rusty but operational blaster. Maybe Luke and Han had trusted their droid to prepare the ships, but Div trusted only himself. It was how he had stayed alive for so long.

"Stop right there!" The feeble command came from a thin, wispy Kaminoan in the entryway of the docking bay. He wobbled on spindly legs and clenched a thin, tattered lab coat around his shivering body. "You're supposed to be dead! I told those Imperials to take care of you!" he shouted, raising a blaster. "I won't let you destroy my experiment!"

"No one wants to destroy your experiment!" Div shouted. "We just want to leave here!" He ducked as the Kaminoan fired a burst of laserfire at him. The shot went wild, and the scientist stumbled backward with the unexpected recoil. The laserfire ricocheted off Div's ship, scoring a shallow gash to the hull. "I don't want to kill you," Div said, drawing his own weapon. "But I'm *not* going to let you damage this ship."

The scientist was insane; that was obvious. But he was a madman with a blaster. Div aimed his own weapon. It was useless, but the Kaminoan didn't know that. He had the scientist in his sights. "Back off," he called out. "Let me take off, and I'll leave you here in peace."

This is risky. Div thought. *Too risky.* Normally, he would have shot him. It would have been the smart move. But that wasn't an option this time. "I'm just going to get on the ship now," he said as he backed toward the Howlrunner, his eyes never leaving the crazed Kaminoan. "And you just —"

Another stream of laserfire shot toward him, this time hitting closer to the mark.

Luke's and Han's ships lifted off the ground. If he didn't move soon, he'd be left behind. "Enough!" he shouted, and squeezed the trigger, purely on instinct. To his surprise, blue-green laserfire spurted from the blaster and slammed into the wall just over the Kaminoan's head. A chunk of duracrete slammed into his shoulder, knocking him to the ground. Div lunged for his ship. Within seconds, he had powered it up and lifted off the ground.

I missed, he told himself. *Maybe the weapon was still faulty after all. It happens.*

But it never happened, not to Div. He'd missed on purpose, saving the life of an enemy. He'd tried hard to rid himself of weakness, of the remaining shreds of mercy and doubt that made life so dangerous. Once again, he'd failed.

Div piloted the ship through the exit of the docking bay. The sky swarmed with TIE fighters. Laserfire blasted by, shattering against the Howlrunner's defensive shields. The ship could take a few seconds of this kind of pummeling, but no more. He had to make it into open air if he wanted to fight back. Div accelerated, pushing the ship as fast as it could go. Behind him, there was a thunderous crash, as if the sky had split open. He glanced back, just in time to see the research station erupt in flame. The Kaminoan scientist and all evidence of his precious experiment were gone forever.

Div forced his attention away from the ground and up to the sky. He was going to have to fight his way past the TIE fighters and out of the atmosphere, or he'd end up just like the scientist: blasted into oblivion.

CHAPTER SIXTEEN

Pull up.
Pull up.
PULL UP!

The thought began as a dim echo in the back of Luke's brain, but within seconds it swelled to a roar. He obeyed the instinct, yanking the controls back hard. The Howlrunner rose in a precarious climb through dense clouds. A TIE fighter screamed past, bare meters beneath him. Flying nearly blind in the storm, Luke hadn't even seen it coming. If something hadn't inspired his change in direction, the two ships would have collided.

Luke let out a thin, shuddering sigh, forcing himself to concentrate. TIE fighters darted in and out of the clouds, sparking the frequent bolts of lightning. The electrical storm was disrupting his radar and jamming the comms. He could only hope the Empire's pilots were similarly disoriented.

Rain slapped at the ship. Winds buffeted him from side to side. The Howlrunner was an Imperial ship, and unlike the X-wings, it had a fixed-wing design, along with laser cannons that were weaker than what he was used to. On the plus side, he could push it faster than an X-wing, and its narrow profile made it a difficult target. But in this weather, everything was a difficult target.

Focus, Luke told himself. Without radar, without a clear line of sight, he had little to go on but his instincts.

And the Force.

Luke dived sharply.

A laser bolt rocketed past. He turned his vehicle and backtracked its trajectory, tearing after the TIE fighter. It spiraled up through the clouds. Luke stayed close on its tail, struggling to keep the Imperial in his sights. The fighter looped to starboard, then climbed sharply to ten thousand meters and disappeared into the gray mist. Luke plunged after it, scanning the horizon for the flicker of light that would give it away. Nothing but cloud and rain — and then a forked bolt of orange lightning flashed across the sky.

There!

Luke squeezed the trigger. A laser bolt sliced through the clouds, straight for the Imperial. A fireball lit the night.

But before he could celebrate, he spotted something out of the corner of his eye. Clouds swirling, as if a huge object was tearing through them. Like a ship.

Luke jerked hard on the controls, executing a gut-dropping pivot so he was facing the oncoming ship. He readied his weapons and —

No!

Something made him hesitate.

He waited, knowing that the other ship was about to have a clear shot. Luke tightened his grip on the weapons trigger, ready to fire at the first sign of trouble.

The vessel emerged from the clouds. It was another Howlrunner. Luke had almost fired on Div.

But why didn't he fire at me? Luke wondered. In the murky skies, it would have been just as easy for Div to mistake Luke's ship for a TIE fighter. Somehow he'd known to hold back.

Maybe he's as good a pilot as he says, Luke thought grudgingly. *Lucky for me.*

Div's ship peeled off from its trajectory and banked shallowly to port. It shot off two short bursts of laserfire, though no enemy targets were in range.

It's a signal, Luke thought. *He wants me to follow him.*

All he had left were his instincts, and his instincts were telling him to trust Div.

So he did.

• • •

Skimming so low over the city that the belly of his starfighter nearly toppled the durasteel spires, Han watched Div and Luke break through the clouds overhead. They ambushed three TIE fighters running recon over the station, picking off the enemy one by one as their ships danced and weaved through a barrage of laserfire. It wasn't just that they were remarkable pilots —it was the way they worked together. With the comms out, they were all on their own, or should have been. But even from where Han was, he could tell that Luke and Div were functioning as a team, one anticipating the other's move almost before it happened.

Good thing that guy's on our side, Han thought.

At least for the moment.

Chewbacca, wedged into the copilot cockpit a few feet behind Han, barked a warning. But Han already saw them: two TIEs, four and seven o'clock. Both hot on their tail. "I see 'em, Chewie," Han said, upping the fore thrusters. He fired a short burst from the tail guns, but the fighters evaded him easily. He had to maneuver behind them, turn the chase around — which meant he needed to shake them or outrun them. "Let's see how fast she can go," he muttered, pushing hard on the accelerator.

They shot forward, the g-forces flattening them against the seats. But the TIE fighters kept pace with ease. A stream of laserfire sizzled past his cockpit window.

Han banked sharply to port as they fired again. A bolt glanced off his wing.

"Blast!" Han cursed, dipping the nose of the ship toward the ground. If he couldn't outpace them, he would have to outfly them.

As the ship lost altitude, the city rose around him. Chewbacca issued an alarmed growl. "I know what I'm doing," Han snapped.

Pushing the ship to breakneck speed, he weaved through the empty Kaminoan streets, guiding the ship down winding boulevards. The TIEs were forced to follow single file. Han whipped around a hairpin turn and ducked beneath a bridge, waves lapping at the belly of the ship. The lead Imperial took a shot, but it went wild, slamming into the side of a building. The laser bolt knocked loose a shower of duracrete chunks, which rained down on the slower of the TIEs like an asteroid field.

Han heard the explosion as the ship crashed to the ground, but he couldn't spare a look back.

The remaining Imperial was still matching him turn for turn, move for move. Han knew he could climb to a higher altitude and try to get the jump on the TIE fighter in open sky—but churning with storm clouds and crowded with enemy craft, the skies were hardly open. At least down here he knew what he was dealing with.

He swept through the city, searching for just the right spot. Finally, he veered around a building to find exactly what he'd been looking for: a long, narrow straightaway ending in a monolithic slab of duracrete. Han gunned the engine and headed straight for it.

I know what I'm doing, he reminded himself, ignoring Chewbacca's increasingly loud protests.

The TIE fighter stayed on his tail, as he knew it would. "Just a little farther," he murmured. "A little closer."

The building loomed before them, too massive and too close in the cockpit window.

Now! Han yanked the controls, forcing the ship into a ninety-degree climb. The ship roared up the side of the building. Han allowed himself a single glance back.

The TIE fighter was almost as fast, but not nearly so lucky. Instead of pulling up, it veered around the building, avoiding it by less than a meter. It cleared the structure — but not the thick, tall levee holding back the sea behind it.

As Han had flown to the sea on the aiwhas, he'd passed this way and been taken by surprise by the levee that appeared out of nowhere, marking the edge of the city. The aiwhas had known enough to avoid it; the TIE fighter crashed right into it. The ship exploded, ripping a huge gash in the seawall. A flood of water gushed into the abandoned streets.

Han adjusted the angle of his climb and accelerated toward the edge of the atmosphere, noting out of the corner of his eye that Div and Luke had taken down the last of the enemy ships and were doing the same. Soon the air thinned out, the clouds faded away, and the cool, crisp glimmer of stars shimmered in the distance, glowing brightly in the vacuum. Han grinned as Kamino fell away behind him. Space was waiting.

And so were four more TIE fighters, holding a low orbit over the planet.

They opened fire.

Luke increased power to the thrusters and accelerated through the atmosphere. The planet shrank beneath him, but he couldn't jump to hyperspace until he was safely out of range. And there were four TIE fighters blocking his path.

"Enemy fighter on your tail," Han reported through the comm.

"I see it!" Luke dropped into a corkscrew spiral. The TIE stayed close, hugging the same tight curves.

"Incoming!" Han shouted, too busy with two fighters of his own to lend a hand. Div was holding his own, pursuing a fighter with scorch marks lining its solar array wings. A trail of smoke streamed from its command pod.

Laserfire streaked toward Luke's ship. He deployed countermeasures and pulled a reverse-S maneuver, flipping his craft upside down and backtracking over the TIE fighter's head. He slipped into the Imperial's blind spot for just a moment, but it was all the time he needed. He locked in the target, squeezed the trigger. A blast of white-hot laserfire shot toward the TIE fighter.

It exploded. The solar array wings blew off and drifted into space.

One down, Luke thought, swooping around to join Han's fight. *Three to go.*

"Blast it!" Han slammed a fist on the control panel. He'd never be used to flying this piece of junk. It might have been more maneuverable than the *Falcon,* and its parts might have been in better working order, but it wasn't *his* ship. The *Falcon* felt like a part of his body; it responded almost before he made a move. The ARC-170 was just a machine. And, as far as Han was concerned, not a very good one.

Chewbacca growled a warning.

"I see it, I see it," Han muttered, peeling off from his trajectory as a fireball whizzed past. A TIE zoomed up from below and unleashed another barrage of laserfire before he could steer out of the way. The ARC's shields bore most of the brunt, but a few bolts snuck through. The alert system went haywire, screaming of damage to the hyperdrive. Han cursed under his breath and slammed a fist into the controls again, silencing the alarm. He needed to focus on surviving the next moment, then the next.

"Think you can sneak up on me?" Han shouted, pushing the accelerator and hurtling past the closest of the TIE fighters. Activating the inertial damping system, then slamming the aft thrusters, he flipped the ARC end over end, reversing direction in a hairpin swivel that put him face to face with the shocked Imperial pilot. "Think again." Han waved at the Imperial, then pulled the trigger. One good thing about the ARC fighter: The laser cannon muzzle was designed to internally tilt the beam, offering a few more degrees of accuracy.

It was a direct hit.

The TIE's cockpit window shattered into a shower of transparisteel as the ship imploded. Caught by the shock wave, Han's ship lurched and shuddered, and he was nearly trapped in the blowback fire of the explosion. But he guided the ship safely out of range, already homing in on the second fighter. "Can't believe that actually worked," he muttered.

Chewbacca barked sharply.

"What are you worried about?" Han said. "Even without the *Falcon,* three of us can take two TIE fighters, easy."

But then he glanced at the radar screen and answered his own question. Another enemy ship was drawing into range. A *larger* ship, shaped like a dagger.

Han shot Chewbacca a worried glance. Two TIE fighters was one thing. Two TIEs and a Star Destroyer was another altogether.

"You seeing what I'm seeing, kid?" Han asked through the comm.

Luke's voice was steady. "Copy that, Han. I'm not giving up yet."

As he spoke, the bank of turbolasers on the Star Destroyer's starboard side swiveled toward his ship. And fired.

Div watched it all happen with a clarity he hadn't experienced in a long, long time.

The laser bolt speeding toward Luke's Howlrunner.

Luke, as if he'd expected the shot before it happened, was already taking evasive maneuvers, shifting hard to starboard and diving away from the incoming fire.

The TIE fighter easing into Luke's blind spot, taking advantage of his momentary distraction. Preparing to fire.

Han was pinned down; Luke was focused on the Destroyer.

Div could watch his target go up in flames, return to his employer, and claim the reward money all for himself. Or he could act.

It was as if the ship had decided for him. Feeling as if he were watching himself from a great distance, Div rotated the vessel, coming up fast and shallow behind the TIE fighter. Just before the Imperial pilot could fire on Luke, Div launched a concussion missile.

Direct hit. The flimsy fighter exploded.

Div dodged and weaved through the flak, soaring over the wreckage — and straight into the Destroyer's line of fire. The Empire's cannon attack strafed his wings and blew out the shield generator.

A hail of laserfire lit up the cockpit. Alarms blared. Hits to the navigation, propulsion, targeting systems. Engine power overload. Port thrusters dead, starboard thrusters firing out of control.

The ship fell into a dizzying spin. The cockpit filled with smoke.

All because I couldn't watch a Jedi die, Div thought bitterly. *Not another one. Not again.*

He'd been weak once more; he'd given in to impulses that should have been long since destroyed. Maybe death was the punishment he deserved.

He waited for the Destroyer to deliver the final blow.

But before it could, a ship jumped out of hyperspace, a rusted Corellian clunker that wouldn't last five minutes against the Imperial onslaught. If it tried to attack the Star Destroyer, it would be a momentary distraction for the Empire's craft, nothing more, before they returned to the task of slaughtering Div and the rest of them.

If the freighter was an Imperial ally, then maybe it would take Div down first. He almost laughed: Imagine the galaxy's greatest pilot blown away by such a sad, misshapen bird. Either way, it didn't matter. Dead was dead, regardless of who dealt the blow.

Div shut his eyes and waited for someone to fire.

"Fire," Leia ordered, hoping that C-3PO had absorbed her quick tutorial on operating the quad laser cannons. Laserfire launched toward the Star Destroyer, scoring a direct hit on its shield generator dome. Leia quickly guided the *Millennium Falcon* out of the Destroyer's firing range and took a quick survey of the situation. Three battered ships — one out of commission, two intact but taking heavy fire.

She tuned the comm to a Rebel frequency, hoping to pick up evidence that her friends were inside. As she did so, she accelerated and hurtled toward the remaining TIE fighter, which was lurking just beneath one of the strange ships, about to fire. Two quick blasts from the laser cannons blew it into debris.

"Took you long enough." Han's voice over the comm was as infuriatingly cocky as ever. Leia allowed herself a short sigh of relief. She'd worried she might never hear that voice again. "But what I want to know is who gave you permission to fly my ship?"

"Excuse me, Your Highness, but the Star Destroyer seems to be powering up its turbolasers again," C-3PO relayed, sounding worried. "At this juncture, might it be wise if we considered perhaps —"

"Just *fire!*" Leia snapped.

"Tell me you didn't let that tin can fool around with my laser cannons," Han moaned.

Leia ignored him. Now that the final TIE fighter had been destroyed, she could concentrate on the Star Destroyer.

When Zev and Wedge had reported back to Yavin 4 with news of the failed mission, Commander Narra had been convinced that Han and Luke were lost. There had been no life signs in the Kaminoan city, no indication that they had survived the crash. But Leia had told herself that electrical storms in the atmosphere could have foiled their sensors — that Luke and Han *must* have survived.

Now that she had them back, she certainly wasn't going to let a Star Destroyer take them away. And fortunately, she didn't have to fight it alone.

"*Now,*" she said into the comm. Eight X-wings, three Y-wings, and a blockade runner emerged from behind the planet. They'd exited hyperdrive on the other side of Kamino, hiding in its shadow while Leia scouted the situation. Now they were ready to enter the fray.

The Rebels opened fire on the Star Destroyer. Laser bolts ricocheted across its bow, and a string of fireballs exploded along its starboard side. The *Millennium Falcon* led the charge, swooping low over the shield generator dome and unleashing a pair of proton torpedoes. The second hit was more than the dome could take. It cracked and exploded, leaving a large swath of the Destroyer's hull defenseless.

The X-wings took full advantage of the opportunity, peppering the ship with laserfire while Han and Luke concentrated their fire on the gravity well projectors — which, if overloaded, could take down the main reactor.

"Han, Luke, are your hyperdrives intact?" Leia asked through the comm. They needed to flee the system before the Star Destroyer released its squadron of TIE fighters.

"Negative," Han said. "But I can hold them off, give you time to get away."

"You're just full of dumb ideas, aren't you?" Leia snapped, trying to cover her panic. There was no way she was leaving this system without Han.

"We're not going anywhere without you," Luke said.

"Don't be stupid!" Han shouted. "You stick around here and none of us make it home."

Leia pressed her fingers against the comm as he spoke. She could feel the vibrations of his voice.

She forced a careless laugh. "You've always said your ship can —"

"Exactly, *my* ship," Han cut in, his voice tight. "And I'm telling you to keep her safe."

"Right now she's busy keeping *you* safe," Leia said, firing on the Destroyer again and again.

They might have enough firepower to take down the

Star Destroyer . . . *might.* Or she might be leading her people to their last battle.

I know what I have to do, she thought, and flipped on the comm, preparing herself to give the order.

But before she could act, the Star Destroyer made her decision for her. Apparently deciding that the Rebels *did* have enough firepower to take it down, perhaps because of orders, it suddenly made the jump to hyperspace.

The Rebels were alone.

Leia realized she'd been holding her breath. She let it out in a whoosh and massaged the muscles in her neck, all of them rock solid with tension. Then she smiled and flicked on the comm. "Well?" she asked Han. "Don't you want permission to come aboard?"

CHAPTER EIGHTEEN

-3PO put his golden arms around R2-D2 and gave him a clanking hug. "I thought I'd never see you again, Artoo!"

They stood in the main hold of the *Millennium Falcon*, waiting for the jump to hyperspace. R2-D2 beeped feebly.

"What do you mean I'm squeezing too tight?" C-3PO asked, letting go.

R2-D2 whistled a long response.

"You told me so? What do you mean you told me so?" The astromech droid beeped peevishly.

"I most certainly will *not* admit that you did the right thing by going on this mission," C-3PO said.

R2-D2 whirred and chittered.

"Well, of *course* I'm glad you were able to save Master Luke," C-3PO admitted. "But that doesn't mean you were right to take all those crazy risks." He crossed his arms. "I'm very disappointed in you, Artoo."

The astromech droid beeped plaintively.

C-3PO shook his head firmly. "Oh, no. I assure you, I would *not* have done the same thing in your place."

R2-D2 didn't reply.

"Believe whatever you want to believe, you bucket of bolts! *I* know how to take care of myself. And you would be smart to follow my example."

The astromech droid beeped, pointing its manipulator arm at C-3PO.

"Me?" C-3PO asked incredulously. "Follow *your* example? Do you want both of us to end up on the scrap heap? No, no, Artoo. I think it's best that from now on, you stay close to my side, for your own safety."

R2-D2 trilled a question.

"Yes, for your own safety," C-3PO snapped. "Why else would I want you around?" He clapped a hand on his counterpart's dome. "Now, let's clean you up. All that rain *can't* have been good for your circuitry."

C-3PO strutted out of the hold, and R2-D2 wheeled happily after him. It was good to be home.

Leia switched over to autopilot. "I'm waiting," she said, glancing back at Han.

"Waiting for me to take over?" Han said, sliding into the copilot seat beside her. "Don't worry, Your Highness, your wait is over."

Leia rolled her eyes. "*Waiting* for a thank-you."

"Thank-you?" Han asked incredulously. "What am I supposed to be thanking you for?"

Leia resisted the urge to frown. Barely. "For saving your life?" she prompted him. "For blasting those TIEs out of the sky?"

Han shrugged. "I had the situation under control."

"Under control?" Leia laughed. "Without my help, you would have been—"

"Help?" Han echoed. "*Help?* All *you* did, Your Worshipfulness, was get in *my* way. You're lucky you didn't get us all killed. Not to mention my ship!"

"What about *your* ship?" Leia asked tightly.

"A busted fuel line, dented warp vortex stabilizers, and a giant hole in the aft hydraulics." Han glared at her. "All because *you* had to fly her into a war zone."

"Silly me," Leia snapped. "Next time, I'll just stay away!"

"Good!"

Leia stood up. She was tempted to shove Han out of the copilot seat. Or out of an airlock. But instead, she turned her back on him.

• "Where are you going?" Han asked, the anger suddenly gone from his voice.

"To find *Luke,*" she said pointedly. "At least *he* knows how to be grateful."

Han flicked a hand, as if waving aside the idea that anyone could be better company than him. "Ah, I can be grateful."

Leia suppressed a smile. Han was so predictable. He couldn't stand the idea that anyone was better than him, at anything. Especially Luke. "Oh really?" she asked skeptically. "Go ahead, prove it."

"Thank . . . you," Han said slowly, as if the words caused him physical pain.

"For?"

"For gifting us all with your royal presence, Princess," he drawled. "For honoring us peasants with your majestic —"

"Oh, stow it, bantha brain." Leia gave up and headed out of the cockpit.

"Leia?" Han said when she was almost out.

She froze, refusing to look at him. "Yes?"

"That wasn't the *worst* flying I've ever seen," Han admitted. "And at least the ship's still in one piece."

It was a good thing she had her back to him, because against her will, her lips curved up in a small smile. "You're welcome."

Luke sat on one side of the freight loading room. Div sat on the other, his wrists tied with makeshift binders.

"Is this really necessary?" Div asked, lifting his bound wrists. "It's not like I can go anywhere, and you can't be worried I'll sabotage the ship. Not while I'm still on it."

"It's a precaution," Luke said.

"I saved your life," Div reminded him.

Luke nodded. "I won't forget that."

But not so long ago, he'd met another stranger who'd risked himself to protect the *Falcon* and its crew. That stranger had been welcomed into the Rebel Alliance, no questions asked. That stranger had betrayed them. Betrayed *Luke.*

They'd started asking questions.

"I also won't forget that you're only here because someone paid you to kill me," Luke said.

"If I'd wanted you dead, you'd be dead by now," Div pointed out. "I could have let the beast take you. Or the Kaminoan. Or the TIE fighters. Or —"

"I know." Luke felt a twinge of guilt. Div was right. He'd protected Luke, again and again, often at great cost to himself. His ship had nearly been destroyed by the Empire. If the *Falcon* hadn't shown up when it did, Div would surely be dead by now.

"Look, I have nothing against you," Div said. "It was a job, nothing more. And it's over now. Just drop me off at the nearest planet and you'll never see me again."

Luke shook his head. "We're not done with you yet."

"Hey, don't start with any nonsense about me joining your ridiculous Rebellion," Div said quickly. "We may have teamed up on Kamino, but that was just so we could get *off* Kamino. It doesn't mean I'm looking for permanent allies. I've learned my lesson about hopeless causes."

Luke was tempted to ask what he meant by that.

But X-7 had pretended that *he* was done with causes, too. He'd invented a tragic backstory to gain their sympathy. He'd let them *convince* him to join the Rebellion. They'd nearly begged him to stay, to fight by their side.

Whatever he did to us, it's because we let *him,* Luke thought, disgusted with himself. *Because* I *was too blind to see the danger.*

Luke had convinced himself that the Force wanted him to trust X-7. But the truth was *Luke* had wanted to trust him. He'd fooled himself. And for that, he had only himself to blame.

"We'll let you go . . . as soon as you tell us everything you know about the man who hired you." Luke kept his voice steady and free of emotion. Whatever guilt or hesitation he might be feeling, he wasn't about to let it interfere.

Div met his eyes, his own gaze steely. "Afraid I can't tell you that. Ratting out your employers tends to be bad for business."

"I know who it was," Luke said. "I just need you to tell me where to find him."

"Not going to happen."

Luke stood up. "Then I guess you'll be staying with us for a bit longer."

"You can't keep me here forever," Div said. "And you won't *make* me talk. You're not the Empire."

"You're going to help me," Luke said as he left the freight room and locked the door behind him. "One way or another."

He hated this. He, Han, and Leia had agreed: They would bring Div back to Yavin 4. But it still felt wrong to imprison the man. Luke pushed down the guilt. It was surprisingly easy. Maybe because there was another emotion roiling in him, a far stronger one.

Anger.

There was an icy certainty deep in his gut: X-7 was behind this. And X-7 wasn't going to stop until Luke was dead. Div might be their only chance of catching him.

Luke's fingers curled into a tight fist. He ground his knuckles into his palm. Just the thought of X-7 sent a hot flood of fury rushing through him. *Enough,* he thought. Enough always looking over his shoulder.

Enough of being hunted.

With Div's help, he would track down X-7, whatever it took. Then he would end this, once and for all. This time, finally, *Luke* would be the hunter.

And X-7 would be his prey.